FOURTH AT JUNCTION

The unauthorised appearance of a CIA agent in London creates concern for the safety of the visiting American President. His presence causes the circumstances surrounding the defection of Kim Philby to be re-examined and finally leads to the identification of the person who warned him to flee to Moscow.

The operations of a special section of the British Security Services evolve against the background of a collection of vagrants, the Beating of Retreat and the operations of the KGB in London.

The involvement of the Prime Minister and his distaste for a President bent on securing his own re-election, irrespective of the consequences for Britain, lead to a way being left open for the attempt on the President's life.

FOURTH AT JUNCTION

by

JOSEPH BARKER

ST. MARTIN'S PRESS
NEW YORK

Library of Congress Cataloging in Publication Data

Barker, Joseph.
   Fourth at junction.

   I.   Title.
PZ4.B2552Fo   1980   [PR6052.A6487]   823'.914   79-28479
ISBN 0-312-30181-2

ONE

The sun was shining fitfully and the wind was blowing up the Thames, as he made his way past the Underground station into Temple Place Gardens. A group of boys who had just visited the *Discovery*, at its berth at the Embankment, were letting off steam, barely under the control of their two teachers.

Floydd was careful not to be jostled as he moved through them. He had not eaten for three days, his tongue was coated and his saliva thick and clotted, his legs were still reasonably strong, but his balance was poor.

He passed into a wider, gravelled area, with an ellipse of seats, on which sat typists and clerks, economising, eating their sandwiches and biscuits and hoping for a prolonged burst of sunshine.

The queue at the far end of the gardens stood still. No movement in their ranks, eyes cast down, mumbling, waiting. Floydd realized that he had never seen men so still, husbanding their strength. Their clothes were infinitely varied; all were unkempt and their shoes invariably showed the irregularity of their existence.

Floydd took his place behind his fellow tramps, dropouts and unfortunates. He was conscious that his mouth was dry and that his right leg ached. If he walked for any distance in these old corded shoes, his limp returned and now he felt a steady throb from the wound, which had healed long ago.

He had heard that the van arrived at half past one, so there was some time to wait and others joined the queue behind him. Floydd felt the warmth of the sun, as it broke through the clouds. He had settled into the lopsided stance in which he could stand for hours.

After eight years, Floydd was able to blot out from his mind all but the pressing requirements of food and shelter; his memories were almost completely gone. His thought process had slowed and the exhausting tension had eased from his system. Often he was totally oblivious of his surroundings and the reactions of those around him. Personal vanity had vanished and only comfort dictated the occasional splashing of water on his weather-beaten face and the scrubbing of his teeth with the stained, splayed toothbrush. His hair still contained some brown, but his beard was totally white.

*   *   *

It was some time before he realized that he had begun to listen to the murmuring behind him. A fight between sparrows at the base of the statue of John Stuart Mill, by which he stood, faded and he heard the words clearly.

" . . . room 667," in a tired voice.

"Out today?" In a sharper voice, which made his stomach contract and forced him to listen, to strain to hear every word.

"No curtains drawn till eleven. . . Why so interested today?"

"Follow instructions, Primrose."

The sharp voice had tightened, now it eased.

"Air Force One tomorrow and Station doesn't know he's here."

" Just interested." The tired voice again.

" Keep it tight, watch until I reach him and keep watch tonight and. . . ."

The rest was lost in the shuffling, muttering and movement forward. At the head of the queue, a van had drawn up. The flap in its side was hoisted and the head and shoulders of a man and woman appeared. Hands were thrust upward.

The woman poured tea into paper cups and the man, two-handed, thrust a pie and a steaming paper cup into the hands of each man, as he moved forward to the side of the van. Floydd shuffled forward, trying to hear more from behind him, but the movement of those around him prevented any intelligible word from reaching him.

He came to the head of the queue, reached up for the pie and tea, his thumb sinking into the bottom of the pie as he gripped it. As he began to thank them, he was pushed aside by those behind him and stumbled, spilling tea and, as he looked down at his steaming coat, the pair from behind him moved past. He limped forward; the inaction in the queue had stiffened his leg.

The two men were heading for a bench and he followed.

The office workers had begun to return to their offices and the seats nearest the queue had been vacated. The advent of the derelicts, bent on enjoying their food and drink, caused the typists to look up, apprehensive that they would come and sit near them.

Many of those from the queue had bundles and plastic bags. In front of Floydd, a man swayed balancing his tea and pie in one hand and, in the other, two bulging, plastic carrier bags crammed with newspapers, foil and all manner of jetsam culled from dustbins and street waste bins. Floydd moved past him and was now directly behind the pair.

They were ill assorted. The taller slouched along in a filthy raincoat, from which protruded dark trousers. The short one wore a jacket, which gave little indication of its original colour and was too long, the cuffs puffed out where he had folded them inward to shorten them. His trousers were brown, of the wide cut of a generation long past, faded and frayed. Though dusty and dirty, their shoes were neither down at heel nor cracked.

Floydd strained to hear their words.

" . . . coming back quite soon. . ." the sharper voice of the raincoat said. The rest was drowned by the sibilance of a jet of water striking a shrub.

On one of the flower beds a stream of urine was being directed by an ancient tramp, who had drunk his tea rapidly, the sudden access of fluid to his system making instant relief essential.

*　　　*　　　*

The message had passed and they separated, the taller moving to another bench.

Primrose sipped his tea, eating methodically through his pie, his eyes cast down, his balding head crossed by long straggling strands of mousey hair. From time to time he cast a rapid look around him. His dirty and unshaven face showed no emotion, but it was clear that he wanted to leave, but could not do so until the tall man had gone.

Floydd sat on the grass, able to observe them both, his head lowered and his hands busy with his meal. It had taken three days to reach London from Luton and, having eaten nothing in that time, he wished to make the best of his pie. First he broke it in two, putting half into the bulging pocket of his overcoat. He carefully broke the crust from

8

the edge of the remainder; it would keep well. This too went into the pocket and he began to take small mouthfuls of the rest. Each mouthful was carefully chewed, the whole process taking five minutes. Then he drank the remainder of the tea, now cold and offering only a flat taste, slightly sweet.

Hearing the voice of the tall man had spoiled his food. The pounding of his heart was partly due to his weakened condition, but largely to the effect of a gripping fear from the past. Scott had not recognised Floydd, but he had not seen him full face and he would not have been prepared for the change in his appearance and features.

To a well-trained eye Scott was not a convincing vagrant. Although his appearance was sufficiently effective to pass in the varied company in which he sat, his eyes were those of a man in his prime, the lanky figure, despite the assumed stoop, was that of a harrier used to daunting exercise over miles of countryside.

His black hair was unkempt, with a touch of grey throughout. From time to time, as he sat on the bench thinking, he straightened from his round-shouldered posture. There was a bulge in his raincoat pocket from his pie, which he had thrust into it and now his hand crushed the empty paper cup.

Scott rose and, without looking at Primrose, wandered past a waste bin, dropping his cup into it and passed on into Temple Place. Floydd followed him, reaching the pavement in time to see him enter a taxi, whose flag was already down. The vehicle made a U turn and disappeared rapidly.

Floydd returned to the gardens and saw that Primrose was not among those in the immediate vicinity.

Floydd tried to ease the whole scene from his mind and

to calm the beating of his heart. He should not have returned to London after all this time. The conversation should have been ignored; he had no interest in the Department's activities and no reason to have followed Scott.

He must relax and let the tension ease, he must forget the whole incident; most important of all he must condition his mind to work at the slower pace. If he could not do this, sleep would be lost to him and all the memories would return to haunt and disturb him, reviving in him the desperation to prove that he had not been involved. That he was not the fourth man.

The sun had reappeared between the clouds and Floydd allowed his eyes to close and his head to fall forward. He breathed deeply and he tried to count his heart-beats, which sounded loudly in his ears.

Numbers began to come to him, telephone numbers, addresses from the past. He began to count his heart-beats to blot out the other numbers.

As the numbers began to go away, his stomach, tensed since he had heard the voice, began to relax and he became conscious of the condition of his mouth again. He felt the thick, white saliva in his mouth. His present condition and the next few hours were all that mattered, he calmed, his head nodded and he slept.

* * *

His head snapped up. A park attendant was making some of those dozing on an adjoining bench move on and they were complaining, cursing him for his enforcement of authority.

As he awoke, he knew that he had not succeeded in closing his mind to the past and had only deluded himself in thinking that he could remain disinterested.

The Eiffel Hotel was the only hotel nearby with room numbers as high as that on its sixth floor. Room 667 would overlook the road, making it possible for Primrose to see the curtains from the road outside. The Eiffel was beside the Embankment and Primrose's disguise would be capable of blending into the surroundings, particularly as he appeared to have been on watch all night.

Again he tried to shut out the questions the conversation had generated and to let his mind go blank. He rose and moved off before the park keeper reached his bench.

He listened to the noise of the traffic as he moved along. Nothing would drag him back into the past, he must blot out the looking back and the looking forward, only the present mattered and his needs were small. The wind freshened, blowing dust into his face, the sun was hidden and there was a hint of impending rain.

His shoes occupied his attention; his own shoes had worn out long ago. His suit had lasted; the tweed was good and now appeared a grey-brown, even the cuffs of the trousers had failed to fray. The overcoat reached only to his knees and was somewhat bulky for his spare frame.

As he raised his eyes he knew he would see the Eiffel Hotel rising ahead of him. He crossed the road to the other side and moved gently along, still some yards from the corner of the hotel.

Numbers jumped back at him. They still had a taxi for their use; they probably still kept it in the mews garage. The registration number of the cab which had taken Scott away was there again; as he watched it drew up in front of the hotel and from it stepped Scott.

Not Scott the derelict. No stubble, fresh-scrubbed, clean-shaven, black hair smooth and devoid of grey. The cream shirt, crimson tie, grey Glen Urquhart suit with the faint brown window pane and the buckskin shoes suggested a man with no business in view.

Floydd knew that he was going to wait.

*   *   *

Primrose, seeing Scott arrive, moved away from the newspaper stand by which he had been watching. He had observed the arrival of Floydd. Though his face had not been familiar to Floydd, the converse was not the case. He had seen his photograph, that of a former member of the Department for whom a watch should be maintained. He would report the sighting to Scott, but from Scott's terse manner earlier, he was in no doubt that to watch his quarry was the first priority. To do that he must have some sleep and change, as he had been up throughout the night and ached in every bone. He moved away, leaving Floydd standing on the corner.

Against the wall beside the corner was the most inconspicuous place from which Floydd could watch. His eyes moved up to the sixth floor.

He began to feel physically ill, then he remembered that he had eaten only an hour before, after a fast of three days and he felt the tenseness dissipate marginally.

It was not the sudden burst of sunlight on Scott's handsome face which brought Floydd's head up in amazement; it was his recognition of the man beside him.

They stood together at the front of the hotel and let the commissionaire summon a taxi. The sun glinted on the white hair of his companion. The soft grey suit, white shirt and plain blue tie of Al Fransen were as typical as the inevitable black shoes.

12

Floydd could not follow, he had no money for taxis and doubted that a cab driver would stop for him. The sight of Al Fransen generated the urgency to move on.

He walked back towards the Embankment, crossed to the gardens below Whitehall, found a vacant bench and sat down, determined to ease it from his mind, to feel calm return. Then he would cross the bridge and find somewhere to sleep near Waterloo Station, start early next day and get away to Kent.

TWO

A drop of water hung suspended on the arch, released and fell into the pool near his feet, another gathered, was held suspended, then plopped into the puddle.

It had rained heavily and for a prolonged period, only easing to the present light drizzle an hour before. It was twilight and Floydd had reached this spot prior to the storm and sat huddled, his shoes preciously dry. He listened to the plop as each drop hit the pool, allowing the noise, the gradual forming of each drop and its detachment from the stone to occupy his whole mind.

He became conscious that his mind was no longer on the pool; the face of Al Fransen came back to him and he tried to exorcise it, thrusting his hand into his overcoat pocket and pulling out the half pie. Again he detached the crust, taking time, breaking it away carefully so that the pieces were as large as possible. Having put the crust back into his pocket, he nibbled at the pie, taking pieces as small as possible, so that the flavour of the meat was brought to his palate to the maximum extent. Finally the pie was finished, he knew sleep would not come, he had used every defence he had, but he could not keep Fransen, Scott and Primrose from his thoughts.

The conjunction of all three was puzzling. Primrose was an outsider, a free-lance, once suspected of working for another security organization and yet he appeared to be

14

operating with Scott against Fransen. Scott had been a member of the Department in Floydd's time, an operator who could be relied upon, maturing well, with the possibility that he would become a top class operative, or even a senior member of the Department. Floydd could not fathom why Scott should emerge from the hotel, apparently on good terms with Fransen, when it was clear that Primrose and Scott were operating against him.

Most important of all, why was the London station of the CIA unaware of the presence of Al Fransen in London? Movements of top agents would almost invariably be reported to the local CIA station and the visit would have its security organised by them. Floydd had not known it was to take place, but Scott had said the President's plane would arrive the next day.

His thoughts were forcing him back, but he knew he should and could take no part in it. His mind would not show him the way through. In any case he could not follow and find out more, his clothes and condition denied him freedom of movement.

At this stage he knew too little to develop a tenable theory, but the sight of Fransen brought back painfully his own anguish, which had led him to leave the whole world of the Department.

*   *   *

Al Fransen had been the head of the CIA team operating in London, investigating the circumstances surrounding the defection of Kim Philby. There had been a furore when Burgess and Maclean went over, leaving behind them a burden of suspicion on those they had known and the disappearance of Philby generated equal heat.

15

In Fransen's view, there had to be a fourth man. Philby had already left the Department, doing only casual work for it, when he disappeared from Beirut. He had become a superb correspondent on Arab affairs, showing an intuitive talent for understanding the Arab mind, which was worthy of his father St. John Philby, explorer, confidant of King Ibn Saud, merchant and businessman. Floydd had wondered how much the father's dominant personality had shaped or twisted Philby's character. Certainly the stammer was a device he could have used to counter his father's influence.

The conviction that someone within the Department had been linked to Philby pivoted on whether Philby went over at a time selected by Moscow, or because he was warned that he had positively been connected with Burgess and Maclean and would be spirited back to London, to be interrogated and put on trial.

From time to time, the Press speculated whether a Cambridge don might have recruited all three defectors, during their time at the university. They certainly were taken into the Moscow network then, but there was no proof that a tutor had recruited them. The trail was cold and unrewarding and the quarry doubtless inactive or dead. Far more important were the questions that had occupied Fransen; had Philby been warned when to go over and who had given that warning?

During his time in London on the Philby defection, Al Fransen had surprised Floydd. They had worked closely together on two occasions before then and he had found the American effective, with a quick mind and a feel for matters in Washington, which was uncanny. Then his principles showed through. In London on the Philby case he had allowed these principles to emerge to the point of

16

paranoia. He was clearly under pressure from Washington, similar to that created by the unmasking of Fuchs, who had passed atomic secrets to Russia, thereby bringing forward the time when Russia had access to nuclear weapons.

Fransen was single-minded in his pressure on the British investigation team and in his own examination of the evidence. Permission was given for him to be involved in some of the interrogations and he also operated independently, running checks of his own, utilising virtually the whole staff of the CIA in London at times.

As a top operative, who in the past year had been handling a desk job, Floydd inevitably came under suspicion, but then everyone did who had known Philby to any degree. All the possible checks had been made on Floydd, he had been exhaustively interrogated by the team and in the last session Fransen had been involved. It was impossible then to believe they had ever been on friendly terms and Fransen took the opportunity to talk with him twice later. Each discussion had been at Fransen's flat and on both occasions Floydd had left when the questions changed to reiterated accusations, hammered home. They were acutely uncomfortable incidents. He had only accepted the invitations because he saw the need to satisfy the CIA, so that he would continue to receive their co-operation in his work.

At forty-four he had almost twenty years of successful field work behind him and the strain had been considerable. The past year had increased this. Although he had not reported it, there had been three incidents which had convinced him that he was on the KGB elimination list.

No operative was safe when he was handling a case and if later he made himself an easy target he could be in danger. The successive attempts, despite his having changed his flat and altered his habits, made him certain that his liquidation was scheduled. There had been no point in putting forward these attempts on his life to Fransen or the investigating team. The attempts had failed and consequently it could be claimed that they were fabricated incidents, designed to clear not kill him.

On his last case as an operative he had been responsible for the death of a Czech girl working for the KGB and he had later found that she had been linked to the head of the British desk of the KGB in Moscow. The romantic attachment and their consciousness of the value of his past experience in his new staff job had been sufficient for him to be marked down.

His limp came from the last of these attempts. A deliberate, late night endeavour to run him down by a car with headlights full on in a deserted street and on the wrong side of the road. Only his leap, as the car hit him, had saved him, but his right calf was badly gashed and the muscle damaged.

He raised himself up, cursing and looked over his shoulder to identify the vehicle. It was the absence of rear lights that convinced Floydd that this was another attempt and that their efforts would continue.

He found himself behaving with uncharacteristic caution, indicating to friends that the greater variety of his wardrobe was vanity and not a desire to avoid recognition.

Some weeks after the Philby investigation was officially concluded, Floydd was called in by James Buckeley, his head of section.

As he settled into the worn armchair in Buckeley's room, he knew Buckeley considered that his recent work was below standard. Buckeley's obsession with lace curtains irritated him. They were the only fairly new and reasonably clean item in the whole room and obscured the view, giving him no alternative but to look directly at his superior. He was giving a final instruction to his secretary on the inter-com, that he should not be disturbed, while Floydd examined the room.

The Department did not receive much in the way of comforts. The carpet was almost threadbare in places, the curtains were faded, their pattern indiscernible over much of their area. The desk was worthy and old, but it had been scored so badly that it would never be restored. Buckeley's books were housed in a cheap teak veneered bookcase, standing beside the safe and the fire-proofed, combination guarded filing cabinet.

The armchair in which Floydd sat was deep and the gap at the back of the seat indicated a total collapse of the springs. He decided that he must appear relaxed and settled back, feeling trapped physically and mentally.

Characteristically, Buckeley's approach was oblique, un-settling Floydd further.

" You know, Clive, it's a great comfort to have a real home to get back to, when you're working on the inside. Gives you a chance to develop hobbies, to lose yourself in family matters, children growing up, their problems and their schools. You find yourself doing jobs a skilled crafts-man would take a fraction of the time to do. Sometimes when I complete a job I spend hours looking at it."

Buckeley was bald, thick-set and of medium height. He was fifty-four, ten years older than Floydd. He was at the limit of the promotion he might achieve before retirement and showing signs of self-satisfaction.

" It's useful being unencumbered when you're in the field, but on the inside it can be a positive drawback. Prob-lems take so much longer to solve and there's not the balm of physical activity to ease the waiting, probing, evaluating, searching, re-examining and sometimes you are forced to conclude that the operation will not achieve a valuable objective. And failures hit hard."

Floydd cleared his throat, but realised that Buckeley expected no answer.

"Clive, you have reached the crossroads. You were one of our top leg men, none of your chums would deny you that, but that does not mean that you could have gone on doing that work forever."

The use of the past tense when applied to his work in the field troubled Floydd.

"Of course, your leg will rule you out of ever being really effective in that role again."

He was closing all the doors before coming to the point.

"You're not happy in the work you're doing at the moment. And it's showing. I wanted to have this talk to hear your view and see what can be done. Few operatives are truly suited to desk work. They don't have the intellectual qualities, the patience and persistence to seek out solutions, to find new initiatives to keep the other side at a disadvantage and to discover the strategy and objectives behind their tactics. Our job on the inside is to make sure we are probing them, not simply reacting. Our objective is hard information on which policies can be constructed and on which political decisions can finally be made by the Minister, by the PM and the Defence boys. But when you're largely desk-bound the strain can be considerable. What's been the problem, Clive? I want to get it out in the open, into perspective and under control."

Floydd moved uncomfortably in his seat.

"These last two assignments have not been easy," Floydd began, realising that this was the battlefield on which his future would be decided.

"Both had the inherent weakness that a vital part of the basic information was incorrect, even though it came from completely reliable sources."

"But you and I know, Clive, that in both cases you aborted the operations simply because you found that the initial hypothesis was wrong. You didn't look beyond and realise that in the second case we had to continue our effort, just to ensure that they didn't realise that we were on to their plans. I know that Harris had been badly hurt in the other operation, but pulling our man out has put our sleeper under pressure and we may have to activate him sooner that we wished."

Floydd was tempted to ask why Buckeley had not intervened and taken control of the operations. However he had to accept that Buckeley had gone over the cases with him at the time and that the decision on the last case had been made by him without consultation. Seconds rather than minutes had been available once he had heard that the operation was built on sand and that their man could be taken. He had not relied on the operative's ability to handle the development.

"We all have to re-evaluate our theories and plans constantly," said Floydd. "I realised that I had been misled in setting up the whole operation. Jenkins is a good man and we knew they could be looking for a pawn to exchange for their man."

"I appreciate all that, Clive, but two in a row and you simply don't seem to be at full stretch. I made a strong case for you to come into this section; I was convinced that you could make the transition.

"I know the Philby enquiry has been unpleasant, but everyone now seems to be happy to let matters rest, except Fransen, of course. I thought you two were on good terms, but you seem to be still on his list. He appears to be determined to prove that there is someone else. I gather he has another couple of candidates, Cambridge men in the Foreign Office, quite apart from you and Emnie."

Far from reducing the tension of the discussion, this served only to increase it. Buckeley was telling him that his credibility was doubted by the Americans. This meant that he was a real obstacle to the Department and the CIA getting back onto a sound footing again. Any defection or treason case was followed by a period in which positive co-operation diminished and only information of minimal value passed from the Americans to the Department or the Foreign Office.

Clearly he was to be the scapegoat on which the sins of the whole community were to be loaded before being placed outside the city wall.

" I am quite certain that I can get things back onto a proper footing with the CIA. Fransen is conducting a crusade. In talking to him a couple of times I have had some inkling of how Alger Hiss must have felt."

He had not explained himself well. The record showed that Alger Hiss was guilty; the suggestion that evidence was fabricated had never been proved. It was no stronger than the theory that Philby's contact was still operating within the intelligence services. Impossible to disprove and difficult to persuade the Press to drop.

" I want you to take some leave, Clive. Get away for a few weeks, longer if you want. We'll cope here somehow. Go somewhere quiet and walk it out of your system. I know how you love the walking and climbing in the West of Scotland."

Floydd felt physically sick. Buckeley was right, in his present condition he did not even have the wit to defend himself. His heart was pounding. This was worse than fear, it was something approaching the terror of the inevitable. The attempts to kill him had established this feeling of inexorability in him, then the pressure from the investigation, the two cases which had gone wrong right from the start and now this. There was no way of talking Buckeley out of it, but he should make some point so that he could establish his right to return to the section and to take up his work again.

" It's probably a sound idea."

His voice sounded weak and he could see that Buckeley had observed this.

" I'll tidy my desk."

Buckeley would know he did not have a current assignment.

"I was offered some deer stalking near Ben Nevis, it should be possible to take up the invitation and I shall contact you in a couple of weeks time."

"Make it more than that, make it more and come back fit. Are you all right for cash? You can have an advance if you need it."

Floydd refused and struggled to his feet from the depths of the armchair, taking Buckeley's extended hand.

" I'll do that, James and I'll leave my contact address with Marjory."

" Look after yourself, Clive."

Buckeley was relieved that a confrontation had been avoided and his objective achieved. The condition of Floydd recently had concerned him and he would come in for some criticism from the Director for leaving him on the last case.

*　　*　　*

23

He left the building, nodding to the security man on the door and headed for his bank. They took an age to confirm the balance of his account as £118 and he drew a cash cheque for £110 and made his way to his flat by bus.

He poured himself a large brandy, splashing in soda. He had skipped breakfast and the drink hit his stomach, driving away the feeling of nausea which had persisted. He looked at what he should take with him and decided to travel light.

His tweed suit seemed the best attire and he changed into it, slipping on thick socks and a stout pair of brogues. He put on his light overcoat and into the patch pockets thrust a spare shirt and pair of socks.

From his wallet he removed his identification papers and driving licence and distributed into several pockets the money he had withdrawn from the bank, together with that which had been in his pocket and in the flat. The cheque book, credit cards and diary he put into a bureau drawer, together with the keys for his flat and the car.

THREE

Floydd awoke; the dull grey of dawn brought back his surroundings to him. The murmur of traffic was the only sound, no birds sang. He ached in every bone of his hunched body. The pool had extended and his shoes were soaked. His feet made a gentle squelching sound as he moved his toes, trying to restore the circulation.

Even when the conscious mind does not function well, the subconscious is capable of sorting through facts and impressions. During his troubled sleep, thoughts and incidents long forgotten were thrown up and placed alongside the incidents of the previous day.

Now he had the key to it all; his mind had cast up the facet of Fransen's diatribe which had startled him eight years before.

" The Communists and your pinko university homosexuals are ruining the whole fabric of Western society. Worse still, your Socialists and the Democrats are steadily eroding the values that made Britain and America great. We shall purge ourselves; McCarthy was a fool to fight so openly. By stealth he could have accomplished far more. Any politician who weakens the resistance of his country to Communist influence must be defeated by any means at the polls or, if elected, silenced."

When Floydd had remonstrated with Fransen, he had drawn on himself all the fire and venom and finally the accusation that he chose to defend his accomplices. This was the second fruitless interrogation by Fransen at his flat. The deep concern which Floydd had felt, had blotted out the memory of the extraordinary outburst, but now it had come back to him.

When he heard of the Kennedy assassination a few months later, the strength of Fransen's statement was already forgotten. Already the calming effect of his vagrant life had removed the need to solve problems.

*　　　*　　　*

He got up, finding it difficult to straighten his back. He flexed his arms and felt in his pocket, locating his stained toothbrush and bent, dipping it into the pool and scrubbed his teeth. The toothbrush was replaced in his pocket and from the other, he pulled out two pieces of pie crust, munching at them, shuffling about, trying to restore the circulation to his feet.

The numbers came back to him and he knew he had to phone Emnie. He looked up at the sky. It would be about half past six. He could only hope that he still lived at the same place. Further up the road was a telephone box and he set off for it, limping painfully. On opening the door, he found to his disgust that a quantity of beer had been spilt in it; it lay on the floor, stale and acrid.

At that hour a reverse charges call seemed improbable to the operator, but he finally convinced her of the urgency of the message. He heard Emnie answer, surprisingly fresh and he agreed readily to take the call.

"Roger, I have to talk to you, I know it's a long time. Are you still at Junction?"

"Who is this?"

Floydd realized that he had not identified himself and

26

that his voice had inevitably altered. His speech was blurred by the damage to his vocal cords, from a blow inflicted in a fight with some meths drinkers and the fact that he spoke little now.

" This is Clive Floydd. I've been away. Can we talk? I know something which could be crucial."

There was a pause and Floydd knew Emnie was wondering whether it was a trap, whether it was indeed Floydd. No one knew where he had been, only his failure to surface in Moscow would have reassured them that he had not defected.

" We'll meet where we were last together," said Emnie, establishing a safe means of determining whether it really was Floydd. Other methods of recognition could have been valueless, as Floydd could have revealed them in debriefing.

" I'll be there in an hour, Clive."

" Fine, I'll see you at the Old Vic, I can make it by then," replied Floydd, pleased that he had not progressed further across London.

" The Old Vic," Emnie repeated, replacing the receiver of the bedside telephone.

*   *   *

Junction is a small department under the control of the Cabinet Office. Its task is to determine whether particular problems are the concern of the Home Secretary, who controls the security and counter espionage activities of MI5 and the Special Branch, or the Foreign Secretary, who is responsible for the intelligence activities of MI6.

At times, Junction was cordially disliked by both departments, but when an operation or problem was unwillingly handed over from one department to another, it was invariably recognised that Emnie ensured a smooth transfer, with information passed over readily and sources adequately protected.

Emnie had been at Junction for fourteen years and had been its head for seven. He was capable of initiating a case and passing it over to the appropriate department and he could also ensure that the necessary weight was given to a problem of which he became aware. His knowledge of the security services was extensive and although he had little charm, his keen mind made him a perfect channel for Floydd.

FOUR

Floydd set off for the Old Vic Theatre, trying to order his thoughts to bring the whole story into a narrative credible to Emnie. His uncertainty regarding the nature of the activity of Scott and Primrose did not make this easy.

He arrived at Waterloo Road far too early and chose to walk on for a while, so that he did not have to stand outside the theatre for too long.

When Floydd returned some time later, no one was there. For a moment he wondered whether something had delayed Emnie. Then he saw him emerge from the car, his small frame thickened by lack of exercise and the lapse of time. He beckoned.

Floydd got into the front seat beside Emnie, who turned towards him, relieved and incredulous.

"My dear Clive, I was wise to suggest a place where few people would be about at this hour of the morning. I would have passed you a hundred times in a crowd without recognising you, but we shall become conspicuous when the traffic begins to pour through."

He let in the clutch and moved off. The Viva was an undistinguished light green. Like Floydd it could have passed unnoticed.

As it gathered speed another car drew out to follow. The bushy eye-browed man driving the Cortina was at pains not to lose the Viva and at times came closer than he would normally have wished.

Emnie swung into the multi-storey car park, collected a ticket, then set off upward, not looking for an empty space, but concerned to reach the top floor where they would be able to see anyone who approached them. As he anticipated, the floor was empty and he parked well away from the exit door to the stairs and lift. He turned to Floydd.

"Have you been in this country all this time? No one could find any sign of you. The whole of the Western Highlands was combed, then the search was extended, but they found no trace of you. The watch on ports and airports was pointless, as Buckeley didn't identify your failure to provide a contact address for three weeks. It finished him."

Floydd listened. It was a great while since anyone had talked to him at such length. To hear these words from someone he had known well brought him an unexpected sense of comfort. He said nothing; he would wait until Emnie was ready to listen.

"Are you going to come back to us? It wouldn't be easy, probably impossible. You've aged and changed. You look sixty, but you can't be much more than fifty. Your beard and hair and those great creases in your forehead add years to your appearance. Is this a disguise, or are you what you seem to be?"

Emnie was talked out. Normally his interrogation technique was perfect. He had learned it in handling prisoners during the war and later used it in his work for the War Crimes Commission.

The ordering of his thoughts stood Floydd in good stead and he began calmly.

"You must understand that I have no direct evidence, but one or two things which happened yesterday have significance when related to a conversation which took place almost nine years ago. Before I begin, you must give me your word that you will not reveal me as the source, or indicate that I am still in this country."

"Provided that no factor emerges later which demands that I identify you, you have my word. You know I cannot give you a complete assurance and I know you will tell me in any event."

A slight edge crept into Emnie's voice in the last few words; the perception of the trained interrogator was obvious, the confident assertion of a man who knows his subject and also the way he is likely to react.

Floydd nodded slightly.

"Fransen is in London, the CIA station don't know, but Scott and Primrose do. They are watching him, but Scott has also contacted him. What are Scott and Primrose doing now? Are they independent or part of the Department?"

"They are part of Chequers Section."

Floydd did not have to be told the significance of this.

*　　　*　　　*

Chequers Section is responsible for the security of the Prime Minister while he is away from London and either at his country home or Chequers, the Prime Minister's official country residence. It has another significance, however. There are occasions when the Prime Minister requires the services of trained men without the Foreign Office or Home Office being aware of the enquiry. On these occasions Chequers Section is used and at times their operations are more than mere enquiries.

*　　　*　　　*

Floydd knew that while Emnie had access to much information of the security services, he would have none on the detailed assignments of CS, even though both Junction and CS came under the control of the Cabinet Office. Too much information must not be in the hands of a single man, no matter how reliable he might be.

" You seemed very wide awake when I phoned, have you been up all night?"

A flash of Floydd's old talent for catching even an experienced interrogator off-guard showed briefly.

" I've not been sleeping well for a long time. When the work load is high, I only manage three or four hours and I lie awake for that last hour, to avoid disturbing Anne by getting up. A few drinks doesn't seem to help and I don't like tranquillisers."

Emnie was relieved to talk for a few moments about a problem which troubled him and which he had not reported at his official annual medical examinations, or mentioned to his colleagues.

" My work goes through, it just takes more out of me when the tougher problems arise."

Emnie brought the conversation back to the point.

" What do you know which makes this so significant, Clive?"

" I was with Fransen twice before I left. He was determined to prove that you or I had been involved in Philby's going over. He would begin by questioning me, then rapidly become angry, talking about the danger to the West of people like me."

" Not the calm Al Fransen we used to know, Clive, but surely there was something more?"

" There were just two pieces more. He reached a point where he condemned the Democrats, saying that Mc-Carthy's error was to proceed too openly and I felt that he

32

was doing more than condemn Kennedy, he was indicating that something should happen to him. All this was in February 1963, before Philby had surfaced in Moscow, but when we were sure his disappearance from Beirut was significant. Kennedy was assassinated nine months later."

" The President is to be on the saluting base at Beating Retreat tonight on Horse Guards Parade. Anne and I are going to watch from the Cabinet Office. Scott being with Fransen disturbs me, but presumably he realizes the danger and that could be the reason for the watch on Fransen. The Prime Minister is a devious old man. Our differences with the United States are considerable, but violent action against a head of state is unthinkable. Scott being with Fransen must have some other significance."

Floydd was relieved. Emnie understood his concern and appreciated the significance of Fransen's outburst.

" I must get to the office, but there is something else I must attend to before I start things moving. Few of us were happy with the report of the commission on the Kennedy assassination. You cast suspicion on a man who once defected to Russia, then have him shot to ensure that the story can never be disproved. Neat, but not totally convincing."

Emnie switched his attention to Floydd. He pulled out his wallet and extracted all the notes, thrusting them into Floydd's hands.

" Take this; I'll try to ensure that you are not identified, but phone me at the office or at home if you remember anything else which could be significant."

Then remembering the reverse charges call, he reached into his trouser pocket and thrust coins into Floydd's lap.

" I don't need this. . . ."

" You need it."

Emnie started the engine and let in the clutch.

" Back to the same place, Clive? Get out of London and away from all this. You were wise to tell me; it may be nothing and Fransen's outburst may simply have been his way of venting his anger at having failed to spot Burgess and Maclean when they were in Washington and right under his nose."

They reached the car park exit, Emnie paid and drove out onto the road. The Cortina, parked between the pedestrian and car exits, started and moved off slowly, following the Viva.

" Try to keep me out of it, Roger. I want to be left alone. It will take me weeks to shake off the stress and get back to the stage I'd reached. It's not an elegant way of life and at times it's hard, but it hurts no one and I no longer have to examine every event for some hidden significance. At the end, I knew the K.G.B. were determined to get me. That car accident was a deliberate running down, everything pointed to it and if I'm picked up the whole Philby connection will start again. It will take ages to establish I've been walking all these years. They will assume I've been away somewhere and have come back after debriefing. Unless they've found the link."

Emnie shook his head, keeping his eyes on the road to avoid seeing Floydd's expression.

" No. Nothing. You and I were the prime suspects outside the FO and small wonder they checked us out. We had access to the information that Philby had finally been positively identified and we both had known that Burgess and Maclean were about to be picked up. It wasn't our fault that picking them up was delayed by the Foreign Secretary. I've never been convinced there was someone, there didn't have to be you know."

34

He drew up at the Old Vic again and held his hand out to Floydd.

" Look after yourself, Clive," he hesitated, " don't tell me which direction you are going in. Get onto a bus or train and get out of London."

" I will, Roger. Thank you for the money, I'll never be able to pay you back and thank you for listening."

Floydd slipped out of the car and began to walk to the corner. He crossed the road, not looking at the Viva.

Floydd walked on towards Waterloo Station and just before it, saw a café, with a steaming urn on the formica topped counter. He went in, ordered tea, fried eggs and bacon and some bread and went over to a small table beside the wall.

From time to time, the man on the other side of the road looked up from his tabloid paper and checked the café door.

FIVE

First thing in the morning, the coffee shop near the Eiffel Hotel caters for those who do not care to make their own breakfast, or have arrived in town ahead of time and wish to postpone starting work until the last possible moment. All are preoccupied with their own thoughts or the food before them.

As Scott and Primrose drank their coffee, the need to avoid being overheard was not paramount.

" Has he moved out at all during the night?"

Scott realised that Primrose could not be positive, as he could not watch all possible exits from the hotel. Scott's resources were limited and the need to watch Fransen rested only on the memory of an old report and the chance discovery that his presence was not known to his colleagues, at a time when British and US security was tuned to a fine pitch for the visit of the President.

" No sign of movement; didn't go out after he returned with you. Drew the curtains just after nine and doesn't appear to have surfaced yet. You had him covered throughout the day yesterday, didn't you?"

Primrose was tired; he had no appetite after keeping watch all night. He had abandoned his thread-bare clothes and wore a raincoat and a suit, which might have belonged to a clerk who had not risen appreciably in his years of employment. He had walked around the area throughout the night, after the coffee shop closed shortly before midnight. He observed with some irritation that Scott was well dressed and clearly had enjoyed a good night's sleep. The desire to obtain promotion to a level where he would control others was strong and he had no means of making his mark other than through Scott; so he must bide his time and make sure that the information he obtained was credited to him.

"Yes I had him in view all day yesterday. Get off home, get some sleep and phone in to the office when you are ready to come back on duty; I don't know how we shall handle this from here on. And make it before four o'clock."

Primrose did not care for Scott's firm tone or the suggestion of sloth on his part and he briefly considered withholding the information he had. However, his desire to shine overcame his irritation and he lowered his voice and leaned forward.

"I saw Floydd yesterday. He's alive and he's grown a beard, but the limp's still there."

"I doubt that very much; he's dead or tucked away somewhere. Our boys have never spotted him here or in Moscow. How could you have recognised him anyway; you never met him."

"No, that's true."

His irritation that his word was doubted and the oblique reference to his relatively recent recruitment into the security services, made him regret having mentioned the sighting to Scott. If he saw Floydd again he would find out what he could before telling anyone, then put in a full report to Trewen, indicating that his original sighting had been discounted by Scott.

"I only know of him, but I did go through the basic files on induction and I know what he looked like from the photographs and description. It was the limp that attracted my attention, his scruffy clothes threw me for a moment, but his interest in your arrival and the way he watched our vehicle clinched it."

" Why didn't you tell me this yesterday?"

Scott was annoyed and he was puzzled by Floydd's reappearance at a spot where surveillance was under way. It complicated the task and threw up all manner of possibilities about this assignment. He wondered whether Floydd had seen him leave the hotel with Fransen.

" Well I'm off, if there's nothing further. I'll put in a report on Floydd and I'll be in touch with the office before four."

Scott did no more than nod in reply, watching Primrose strut to the door. It was a little after nine and the coffee shop was emptier.

Without realising that his black coffee was now cold, he drank the remainder, swallowing it with a grimace of distaste. He left the coffee shop, waited briefly on the kerb, crossed the road and entered the Eiffel Hotel, making for the row of telephone booths with their acoustic hoods.

He dialled rapidly, letting the phone ring twenty-two times before ringing off, having kept his eyes on the foyer. He dialled again and was answered almost immediately. His message was brief, asking to be phoned back at that number or that of the booth alongside and waited.

When his chief phoned back, Scott explained the new development and Trewen decided to have Therfield added to Scott's team, denuding Chequers Section of all their top men.

Scott went over to the hall porter, took a newspaper and settled in an armchair in the foyer.

SIX

Within the Cabinet Office, a senior member of the staff is responsible for advising the Prime Minister on security matters. He acts as a link with the Home Office, MI5, the Foreign Office and MI6 and maintains contact with the Ministry of Defence, which assembles valuable information from Service sources, including the defence attachés in the embassies overseas. Finally he is responsible for Junction and Chequers Section and ensures that CS is available to carry out investigations for the Prime Minister, or on rare occasions to act directly on the Prime Minister's instructions on matters where speed or secrecy exclude the possibility of involving the appropriate ministry or security organisation.

Charles Trewen found his security work both interesting and a trifle frustrating, but in any event it formed only a part of his total duties. He enjoyed active control, but found his function was largely advisory, this control being limited to CS.

The security role had been assigned to him in addition to defence matters and it was in the latter field that his strength lay. During the war, his career in the RAF had been almost totally concerned with photographic interpretation. He had proved himself to be brilliant in that developing sphere, which lay between a science and an art, a fine blend of imagination and selective assessment.

*   *   *

Trewen had already called for the file on Floydd when his secretary told him that Emnie wanted to come and see him. He agreed that Emnie should join him immediately and had time to glance at the first pages of the Floydd file before Emnie arrived. They had a sound relationship based largely on their office connection, but official functions sometimes brought them and their wives together and they met socially from time to time. Trewen found Roger Emnie sound in his opinions, effective and tactful in his work, a pleasant fellow guest and a considerate host. He had suggested to Roger that he should bring Anne along that evening to the Cabinet Office, so that they could watch Beating Retreat from the windows which overlook Horse Guards Parade.

As he sat relaxed in his chair, he knew that Emnie would not have asked for an immediate discussion were something important not in view.

" You look tired, Roger, not sleeping well ?"

" No problems, Charles, sleeping soundly and getting a full eight hours whenever possible. I would never have made a great general, they're supposed to be able to sleep in any conditions and cope on cat-naps for days on end."

" Good to hear it, Roger. If the ability to drop off anywhere is the sole quality required by great commanders, I'm certainly coming nearer and nearer to that ideal."

Trewen moved from the exchange of pleasantries to the matter to be discussed.

" What has come up in the last few hours ?"

Emnie dealt with all the jurisdictional decisions of Junction without reference to Trewen, unless a row were brewing, a major problem arising, or he had come into possession of information of substantial significance.

40

" There appears a real possibility of an attempt on the President's life during his visit to this country."

" Is this a deduction from valid information or simply an opinion which has been passed on to you?"

" Neither really, Fransen of the CIA is in this country as you know. He is here without the knowledge of the CIA London station."

" You already appear to be aware of my knowledge in this area."

Trewen felt a trifle irritated. It was uncharacteristic for Emnie to come to him seeking to elicit information on an operation and very unusual for him to check out the activities of CS. He allowed Emnie to continue.

" Fransen operated very successfully with us over a considerable period. More recently contact has been very limited, partly because he has been assigned to another section, but principally because he was known to have blown his top and become emotionally concerned over our security lapses in preventing leakage of atomic and defence secrets."

Trewen nodded and clearly wanted Emnie to continue.

" While in this country during the Philby enquiry, he talked in a wild manner about Communists, fellow travellers, Socialists and the Democrats. He was in Dallas when Kennedy was assassinated nine months later and had earlier said that something should happen to him. Now he is in London and not under the control of the CIA locally. I believe you must know most of this, but you may not have heard about his outburst against subversive elements in America and the strength of his conviction that they should be eliminated by any means."

" You appear to have one source for both pieces of information, Roger. You must tell me who it is."

Trewen leaned forward, his normally mild features transmuted to a compelling expression as he made the demand.

Emnie shook his head firmly.

" It would not add greatly to the information which you must have and I believe there would be no value in revealing the source."

" You must tell me and you may leave it to me to decide whether the name goes further."

Emnie sat very still; he could trust Trewen, but he wanted Floydd to be left alone.

Trewen placed his finger-tips on the file and pushed it very gently across the table. Before it came to rest in front of him, he had already guessed whose it was. Something had happened of which he knew nothing and he was doubly glad that he had come to see Trewen.

" How is he and how did you make contact with him?"

He had observed the easing of tension in Emnie, when he appreciated that he could be frank with him and was not breaking faith with Floydd.

" He telephoned me at home early this morning and I had a meeting with him. He's in reasonable health and he's been roaming around the countryside. I am reasonably certain he has not been in contact with or under the control of the other side. He found out about Fransen by chance, through Scott's liking for disguise, which he always said was theatrical rather than effective. He heard Scott and Primrose talking."

Emnie deliberately held back the fact that Floydd had seen Scott and Fransen together. If CS were involved in an operation with Fransen or the CIA, it would be top secret and that would lead to a determined search for Floydd, in case he appreciated the significance.

" He is a vagrant, I gather. What you have not told me

42

is whether he will be in contact again and is continuing to track Fransen or even Scott or Primrose."

"You're quite right; he is a tramp and he is probably well away from London by now. I pressed him to leave and I think he may have gone. This would tie in with his having phoned me; that was a needless risk if he felt inclined or competent enough to handle this himself."

"Without any money he might have been unable to handle it, but knowing you, Roger, I'm certain he now has the majority of the cash you had on you. That could make the difference. However, if your view is correct, then he need not represent an embarrassment to us; unless he chooses to interfere in our plans or actions. I presume he had no idea when the attack on the President might be made?"

"No, but I mentioned Beating Retreat tonight."

"I see, then we must keep our eyes open for him."

It was clear that Trewen was not going to tell Emnie how he had become aware of Floydd's involvement. His concern for his defenceless, troubled, former colleague made him feel he must know as much as possible about the circumstances.

"Why did Scott and Primrose not bring Floydd in, surely they could have arranged for that?"

"Primrose saw him, but did not report the sighting until this morning and he might not have been in a strong position had he interfered with Floydd. One could wish that he had at least determined where Floydd was going, but then so could you, I suppose, Roger."

"Do you intend trying to locate Clive Floydd?"

"I shall have to think about that and a number of other matters. An immediate search might not be feasible and there could be little point in looking for him after Beating Retreat tonight."

Emnie felt relieved that there was a possibility Floydd might be able to get away and resume his life, undisturbed by the events which might now take place.

SEVEN

As he was shown into the Prime Minister's study by his Private Secretary, Trewen could hear Big Ben begin to strike the half-hour; already it was ten-thirty and the time at their disposal was small. The sound of the chime was cut off by the closing of the acoustic door behind him. He advanced to the desk and the Prime Minister looked up from a draft speech, into which he had been inserting some characteristic touches. Whether in power or in opposition and no matter how well drafted or how near his style, he found these additions vital in ensuring that his personality dominated his speeches and by inference the affairs to which his words alluded.

He motioned Trewen to a chair.

" I understand that something important has arisen. Please be brief, Charles, two ministers are waiting to be called."

At the beginning of a meeting the Prime Minister liked to demonstrate his touch and memory by using a Christian name. His hands were folded together over the speech, as though he was determined to ensure that they did not fly out in a dramatic gesture during the discussion. Trewen noted the brown blotches on his hands, which were surprisingly smooth for a man of his age.

His fair hair was almost white, very fine and now providing little protection for the substantial dome of his head. He was of medium height and comfortable proportions, which suited his projected image as a father figure and man of the people and also his appetite. The genteel poverty of his early life had required that nothing be wasted and the habit of his youth had been carried into later life, causing him to finish without thought that which was on his plate, whether at a luncheon, a banquet, or in his rooms alone in No. 10.

While his clothes had improved marginally since taking office, this clearly was a day for an opposition suit, which fitted neither at the shoulders nor the waist.

The voice was slow and measured when under control, betraying little emotion and no perceptible accent when used here or in the House. Electioneering and speeches to the unions and the faithful were a different matter; then his Yorkshire accent was brought into play and his words salted with touching phrases from the dialect of his youth.

" Prime Minister, I have placed CS on an active footing to check out a senior CIA operative, who is in this country without notice to us, or the knowledge of their London station."

Trewen kept his comments as succinct as possible, hoping that a detailed discussion would not develop.

" Why does this concern you, Trewen. The President arrived at their base at Lakenheath this morning and the Foreign Secretary has told me that the number of CIA agents over here is substantial."

" The others have been advised to us, this man is not in the European section of the CIA now, he has shown himself to be hostile to our security services, he dislikes Democrats and Socialists and subscribes to the objectives of Senator McCarthy. He was in this country on the Philby investigation eight years ago. I believe the CIA would not have decided lightly to send him over and I am convinced that his declared attitude to our security deficiencies would have demanded that the CIA should tell us of his being sent here."

" This is Fransen, Trewen."

It was not a question but a statement and his eyes, old and faded to a grey-blue by his seventy years, were hard and sure, as he spoke.

" You need not be surprised, you will remember that I was at the Foreign Office at the time and took a keen interest in the investigation conducted into that lamentable affair."

The bitterness that he had been forced to accept some measure of responsibility and that he felt he had been let down by the established system, showed through very clearly.

" I fear an assassination attempt on the President during his visit. Fransen's comments about Democrats preceded the Kennedy assassination by only nine months and I believe he may have been in Dallas at the time."

" I assume you were not convinced by the Warren Commission's report on the killing of President Kennedy. I can understand that view, particularly when one takes into account the subsequent killings. Have you any inkling when the attempt could be made?"

" None, it is for this reason that I have had some checks made on Fransen's movements and Scott of CS has spent some time with him, to demonstrate that we are aware of his presence. We shall try to keep someone close to him at the vital moments, but we already know that the President refuses to be bottled up by security precautions and values being seen with and being cheered by the people of other nations, on the television screens in the United States. I understand that the President may be on the saluting base at Beating Retreat tonight and I recommend that you persuade him to watch from a vantage point or on television."

None of the implications was lost on the Prime Minister. It would be an occasion when he would not be clearly seen on television or by the crowd. Consequently he was confident he could persuade him to watch from the Admiralty. That could be mooted later in the day, when he visited the President at the US Embassy at four o'clock."

" Why has the suggestion that Fransen might be involved in a plot arisen only now? Presumably you have access to new information or a valid new source."

Trewen knew only too well the astute and active mind of the Prime Minister and his irritation when he considered he was being baulked by an evasion.

" Floydd has surfaced and advised us of the potential danger."

" Very well, tell the CIA that Floydd is around, you have no time to handle him and it could be a useful counter if an embarrassing situation develops with the CIA. Try to determine whether they know of Fransen's presence, but do not ask a direct question at this juncture."

Trewen nodded, and felt sure that Floydd would not be allowed to remain untouched by these events.

"Don't interfere with Fransen, but keep a watch on him."

The Prime Minister reverted to the language of the classroom, where his political ambitions had been developed.

" It's a quaint equation. The President's policies will have a disastrous effect on our economy and do not accord with this country's long-term interests. Yet here we have a member of the CIA prepared to remove him in favour of a far more tractable Vice-President, who would probably suit us far better and no one would be able to blame us, particularly if this is part of a long-term plot. It would be tempting to do nothing."

The Prime Minister paused for several minutes before continuing.

"Watch him and report to me this evening. The President will watch from the Admiralty or not at all. I shall not mention a possible plot by one of his own men; to do so might lead him to feel that our attitude to the CIA may be one of suspicion and we must avoid misunderstandings."

As he finished he looked down at the speech and unclasped his hands. Trewen knew that the discussion was over. He was certain the Prime Minister would never initiate the assassination of the President, but he wondered whether the devious, old man would allow the President to die.

"Thank you, Prime Minister, I will provide you with any news this evening."

The old man depressed a button on his desk and his Private Secretary saw him out, before returning for his instructions.

"Have a paper produced which identifies the changes of policy which might be pursued were the Vice-President of the United States to succeed the present incumbent. You may have included in it, identification of his particular strengths and weaknesses, the degree to which he relies on the opinions of his advisers, the extent to which he may mould his policy to meet the needs of his allies. I also wish to know whether he was involved in any deals in return for his place next to the President and whether, as a State Governor, he made excessive use of patronage as a means of securing election, or whether he indulged in the diversion of funds from that campaign to his subsequent presidential campaign fund."

In response to the mild look of enquiry from his Private Secretary, he shrugged off his unexpected request.

" I simply wish to know the kind of man I might be dealing with, as he could succeed the President and it is no bad thing to look at these possibilities, no matter how remote or unpalatable they may be."

" I fully understand. I presume you would wish to have this tomorrow."

" Most of this will already be on file. I would therefore like it in my hands by ten tonight. It will be an interesting document to read after my discussions at the embassy today. Now, please arrange for the Foreign Secretary and the Chancellor to join me in ten minutes. When they arrive, you may take this speech."

The Prime Minister contemplated the prospect of the next twelve hours. He had been expecting the President's visit to be tough, but a new element had emerged and he felt more confident than he had for several days.

EIGHT

On his private line Trewen spoke through a similar link into the office of Mike Stone. He was head of the CIA station, exceptionally bright, only thirty-five and an excellent organiser, as has been confirmed by his handling of the security arrangements for the President's visit. Above all he was prepared to call for help when it was needed and the volume of CIA men in London bore eloquent testimony to this. This and his fear of the presidential walk-abouts and glad-handing. Politicians must be seen to be in touch with the people and totally accessible, no matter how remote from the truth appearances might be.

Mike Stone was the complete antithesis of the typical American in popular imagination. He was short, only five and a half feet, his brown hair cut to reasonable length, bushy eyebrows enhancing rather than shadowing his clear blue eyes. Stone was thick set, but moved with surprising ease and vigour and his mind was as agile as his body.

" Mike, I know you have a lot on, but I need five minutes. I think you will be interested."

" Surely, Charles. I can keep in touch and it's resting time right now."

Trewen knew that this meant that the President was safely in residence at the US Embassy and that he would remain there for some time. Each man had switched in the scrambler on recognising the other's voice.

" How about St. Margaret's, Westminster."

" Sounds fine to me. I'll be there in fifteen minutes."

Stone looked at his watch, realising that he would have to be there by eleven o'clock. He warned his deputy of his absence and as he sat in the car, he wondered what Trewen could have for him. Trewen was not a normal contact. They had met and talked no more than half a dozen times and the arrangements for the President's visit were not Trewen's province, his liaison having been with the Special Branch.

*　　*　　*

Trewen and Stone did not shake hands when they met. They walked slowly and talked quietly, but without introducing the carrying sibilance of whispers.

" Clive Floydd has surfaced. He disappeared from MI6 eight years ago and has been seen in London in the past twenty-four hours."

" I remember the man from my induction to this station. A first-class man who opted out, or the fourth man, if you believed Fransen."

Stone had introduced Fransen's name as Trewen had hoped.

" Surely Fransen's interest is historic, he was in another section when I last heard of him. I understood he'd had enough of this country."

" Right. Now, why are you telling me this?"

" Because you will find out anyway, because your people were very interested, even though we thought you were wrong."

" And?"

" We've been told you have a small operation you have just set up in this country. One man, operating independently."

Stone hesitated for a moment, stopped and turned towards Trewen so that they could see one another's faces in the variegated light which filtered through the stained-glass windows.

" If you are asking whether Floydd is one of our men on an operation, the answer is no. There's nothing you don't already know through channels; it's far too important that nothing goes wrong with Air Force One here. Have you spoken with Floydd; where's he been? Where did you get this small operation from anyway?"

" Stray information from a foreign intelligence man we know. I believe Floydd has been lying up and has not been anywhere sinister. We have not spoken with him and don't know his precise whereabouts, but he was seen in London."

" Where was he seen?"

" Near the Embankment."

" Anything else?"

Stone was sure he would hear nothing further and was anxious to return to the embassy.

" Nothing, I'm afraid."

*   *   *

Having checked that nothing significant had occurred during his absence which could upset the presidential plans, he called for Rod Starker and the Floydd file. Starker had been assigned to London station for over ten years and was approaching the point where he would have to leave the CIA if he again refused a posting to the United States.

The file and Starker arrived at the same time.

" Do you remember Floydd, the man Al Fransen thought was the fourth man?"

Starker responded by providing a detailed account of the case, while Stone checked through the file, interjecting to clarify or supplement certain aspects. When they had examined the salient points, Stone shut the file and leaned back in his chair.

" Where do you think he went to, Rod ?"

" Not to friends; he was low on them outside his work and he had no close relatives. There's never been a trace of a link with Moscow and he's certainly not surfaced there. They could have killed him, but I think we would have heard about that by now. For my money, he opted out. One of our old agents once told me that in this business you're like a whore and her pimp. If the pimp rejects the whore, she's got nothing left. Fransen and maybe MI6 showed they didn't trust Floydd and he split."

" That's possible. Now where are we likely to find him. He was seen in London yesterday by his old employers."

" Not at his flat. He lost that a few months after he left and MI6 took away his possessions, so there is nowhere to go back to. Old friends in MI6, very doubtful, he would only embarrass them and by now he would have been taken in. This sighting without them having questioned him, suggests he has not looked up his old chums. Eight years is a long time. He only appeared to have at the outside £500 on which to live, unless he was able to assume a completely new identity, or was funded by another country.

" For my money he's clean, has been seen by chance and is low on cash. At fifty-two, he would be grey, depending on his condition, he could have whiskers and he's unlikely to have shaken off his limp."

" That sounds reasonable. Get some prints made up, with and without whiskers, showing the ageing and the greying and a physical description. Leave the clothing blank, but

54

indicate a wide scope, except the way-out trendy stuff. Circulate this to all staff attached to us at present. If he is found, he's to be taken to our safe house in Hendon. You will be contacted and you will go there and conduct the first phase of debriefing. We don't tell any of our British contacts we have him until I say so."

" Fine. I'll get right to it and hold over any other work to get this on the road."

Starker was one of the few CIA men without some part to play in the presidential visit.

" And stay with it. I want you to keep in contact with the office, but follow your nose and see whether any of your informants have seen anyone like this."

NINE

The bulky man with bushy eyebrows had an equally thick-set companion, but he was a good deal taller. They had Floydd well in hand and were discussing their priorities.

" I shall finish Floydd," said the shorter. " But first we need to know who he has been working for and why he has been in touch with Emnie."

" Run no risks," said the other.

" My instructions are clear, Siv, but we must try to find out what we can and I want to know what he is up to. That contact with Emnie could be the setting up of another link."

" Do you know where the information came from that he had surfaced? That could give us some ideas," said Siv Ravosky.

" My source gave no indication and we were damn lucky to have got here in time."

" Is it possible that he has been with us for the past few years and we are now liquidating him to prevent him telling anything, while embarrassing the British and possibly the Americans by doing it right here in London, with an important visit in progress."

" I do not think he's been with us. The instructions to kill him on sight have been on file for almost ten years and are always on review. Only today have they been varied, to give us a few hours to find out where he's been and who he's working for."

Nikki Kvist was a top operative in the KGB. Officially he was third cultural secretary in the Russian Embassy, but his title in no way related to his true activities. He had failed to become *persona non grata* only because he had covered his activities well and had avoided violence to an unusual degree. His past record had been as an undercover man and had included operations in the Near and Middle East. Speed, violence and total reliability had been his trade-marks, the violence suggesting an active pleasure in sicken-ing butchery. For a period before his arrival in London, this characteristic had been absent and it became the growing conviction of MI5 that he was now acting as senior security man at the embassy.

*　　*　　*

" Maybe the order was kept out as a cover, Nikki and a means of ensuring that, if he got away from us, he would never be retaken by the British and debriefed."

" You mean in case he was a triple not a double agent? I don't read it that way. I know the man who initiated the order to kill and I'm sure he would have made Floydd's life intolerable and there would have been no possibility of escape."

Nikki gestured with his head, indicating the end of the conversation and that Siv should return to the car. They must not be seen together in the open more than was abso-lutely necessary.

He raised his newspaper, but made sure that his eyes were frequently on the café door. Three workmen came out and just as the door began to swing back behind them, Floydd emerged.

He folded his newspaper and moved off matching

57

Floydd's pace on the other side of the street. He watched Floydd hesitate for a moment as he approached the station. Then Floydd moved forward to the newsvendor at the foot of the steps leading up to the station and bought a newspaper, beginning to examine it as he stood beside the wall.

It appeared to be the *Daily Telegraph* and Nikki tried to identify the page he was reading. It seemed to be towards the centre of the paper and Nikki resolved to buy a copy at the next opportunity.

Nikki could not easily contain his impatience as Floydd turned to pages two and three and continued to read. He watched Floydd fold the newspaper and thrust it into his pocket, with a finality that suggested that it had yielded the information he had sought.

Floydd moved away from the wall, climbed the steps leading to the station and walked over to the men's toilet. Nikki went to the bookstall opposite and bought a copy of the *Daily Telegraph*. He maintained his watch on the exit from the lavatory and turned to page two. Having examined the major news items, he turned to pages fourteen to nineteen. Eighteen and nineteen were business news. Sixteen comprised the leaders and the letters to the editor, fifteen was the woman's page, fourteen the Court Circular, Forthcoming Marriages, Personal Column, Exhibitions and religious articles. Only page sixteen contained news and he could identify no item common to that page and pages two and three.

Not helped by the need to make his check on the paper rapidly, Nikki put the paper under his arm. He was relieved to see Siv hurrying over to him.

" Is he leaving London? Did you hear where he was getting a ticket for?"

" I don't think he's leaving, somehow. He's in the lavatory; that's the only way out. Here, take this paper. He was reading pages two or three and looking at something in the middle. See if you can find a subject mentioned in both places. Watch from over there."

Siv moved away, beginning to examine the pages as he went. Then he took up a position near the exit for the taxi rank, where he could see Nikki and be able to move off rapidly to retrieve the car.

Floydd emerged from the men's toilet and Nikki glanced up at the station clock, he saw that it was almost nine o'clock; as yet he had no inkling of Floydd's plans or his next move. He could only continue the watch for the time being.

He was in no doubt that he would be back in Russia very soon. Floydd's killing would be followed by his prompt departure and a sound commendation might provide the promotion to the interrogation team which he wanted.

Siv had disappeared to get the car and he hoped that he had worked systematically through the stories on the pages he had suggested.

Floydd passed out of the station into the sunlight and shortly afterwards Nikki followed, blinking as he too had to adjust to the glare from the sun. He paused, then located Floydd heading for the bridge and waved Siv alongside, opened the door and told him to move over.

" You take over following him. Leave the paper with me. I will park and go over it; unless you've found the link."

" No. Nothing."

" Right, take the bug and I will pick you up later and locate you through the bug. I should not be more than half an hour."

Nikki started the Cortina and they passed Floydd, who was walking on the left-hand side of the bridge. Nikki stopped at the far end and dropped Siv, who had pinned the bug inside his jacket, having taken it from the glove compartment.

Siv stood outside the shop at the corner of the Strand and watched Floydd coming towards him, nearing the end of the bridge. Floydd suddenly turned left and began to go down the steps leading to the Embankment. Siv moved quickly round the corner into the Strand, then turned left again and walked briskly, seeing Floydd cross the road just ahead of him. Siv fell in behind him and let the gap between them increase to forty yards.

" Embankment, passing Charing Cross Underground Station," said Siv into the bug, " proceeding south."

Floydd continued along the Embankment, walking slowly and pausing occasionally to watch the river traffic on the Thames. Clearly he was in no hurry.

" Passing Westminster Station," said Siv, half an hour later.

Floydd turned right, crossed Parliament Square and went on into St. James's Park, sitting down on a wooden bench, in view of the passers-by as they walked along Horse Guards Road.

" Seated in St. James's Park, beside road, opposite King Charles Street."

Siv wondered when Nikki would rejoin him and moved further into the park, to observe from a distance.

* * *

When Nikki arrived, Siv saw that he no longer had the *Daily Telegraph* with him.

" What is the answer, Nikki?"

" Your last message gave me the clue I needed. I didn't

expect to find it in the Court Circular, but it announces that the President of the United States will be in the official party at Beating Retreat tonight."

He could see that Siv was puzzled and elaborated.

" It will take place on Horse Guards Parade tonight, just across the road from here. The item on page two was a report on a Press conference given by the President before he left Washington and a note on the strong security arrangements being made by both governments, to ensure his safety."

" Why would he be interested in the President's visit? We could be attaching too much importance to him buying that newspaper. He could be here for a meeting with Emnie or someone from one of the ministries over the road."

" We must keep him under observation for the time being. This interest in the President is strange. Could we have persuaded Floydd to act against him?"

Nikki continued with his train of thought in silence, then told Siv his decision.

" I am going back to the embassy. Keep him under observation. If he leaves here, follow him and make contact with the embassy, otherwise wait here till I return."

Nikki saw no alternative to a signal to Moscow to check Floydd's status at senior KGB level.

TEN

When Floydd had been with Emnie, leaving London had seemed the sensible course, if he wished to remain free and untroubled. He had walked towards Waterloo Station and only the sight of the café had deflected him from his intention.

As he sat eating his meal, he wondered whether he could withdraw from the vortex into which he was being irresistibly drawn. Had he failed to hear the conversation between Scott and Primrose, he would have retained the composure it had taken him so long to attain, after the constant pressure of the previous twenty years. Now his desire to know whether his suspicion of Fransen was justified was gaining the upper hand.

One part of his mind regretted his involvement and the loss of his complete indifference to what was happening around him, but now he also felt an overpowering desire to know the outcome.

So great was Floydd's preoccupation with his problem, that he failed to take pleasure in the first warm food he had eaten in several days. The noisy gathering of his empty plate and cup made him conscious that the owner wanted him to leave.

Having determined that the President was attending the ceremony that evening, he decided to clean up a little and went to the lavatory at the station.

As he walked over Waterloo Bridge, he was in doubt whether to turn left or right at the far end. Left would take him to Horse Guards Parade, right was to the Eiffel Hotel, Fransen, Scott and Primrose. There were twelve hours before the ceremony that evening. He could be in the area early and able to secure a position from which he would have a reasonable field of vision. The sun was shining and passing the day in St. James's Park was a pleasing prospect.

Floydd's mind went back to the scene at the Eiffel with Scott and Fransen apparently on good terms. The possibility that CS were acting in concert with Fransen and would provide access to an official building came to his mind. They might be watching Fransen only to make sure that he went through with the attempt.

Finally, Floydd decided that Fransen would use a rifle, probably collapsible, with an infra-red sight, fired from a position on the park side, to one side or other of the Guards Memorial.

By now Floydd had arrived at St. James's Park and he sat for a while, before examining the possible vantage points from which he and Fransen could observe the saluting base.

The sun was warm. The breakfast had provided a sense of well being and an unaccustomed need to digest a meal of reasonable proportions. His stomach had shrunk to a smaller size as his food intake had reduced and he felt uncomfortable. He knew that he had plenty of time. His head nodded forward and he slept.

When he awoke an hour later he felt far better and decided to move about a little. He must not remain in one spot for hours on end; Emnie's office was only a stone's throw away and if he had revealed the source of his information, they could be looking for him now.

To one side of the Guards Memorial was a pile of

wooden hurdles six feet high; this was an ideal place for him. He was sure Fransen would consider access to it too easy for others and reject it. Floydd decided to make use of it himself, getting up on top after the crowd had begun to gather. One advantage of his appearance was that few chose to be in close proximity with him.

The trees presented the best cover for Fransen, other than the memorial itself and for a moment the fantasy of Fransen, dressed in a stone-coloured uniform holding a rifle and standing upright and still on the memorial beside the statues, flashed across his mind.

Both he and Fransen were likely to be on the same side of the parade ground, possibly with the memorial between them. It would make it less likely that he would spot Fransen, but equally it would be safer for him.

Floydd walked away towards the water and stood watching the varied species of ducks, wondering which were there from choice.

He realized that he had something in common with the ducks which had clipped wings. If he were a free agent he would now be on a train or bus, heading out of London.

Floydd settled down on another bench and heard Big Ben strike four o'clock. He felt little excitement as the time passed and the ceremony drew nearer. He almost convinced himself that he was now recovered in mind and capable of resuming his old life and occupation, but he had to admit that he was now old; he no longer had fast reflexes and would be at the mercy of any reasonably skilled operative. Now, after years of discomfort, undernourishment, even starvation at times, he might as well be seventy, not fifty-two.

The sounds of equipment being moved into place aroused him. Guardsmen in khaki, who would not take part in the ceremony were moving the metal barriers, so that those standing on the park side would be prevented from crossing the road and those entering the stands forced to show their tickets.

Floydd decided to take a look from the top of the hurdles, before taking another walk to the lake.

ELEVEN

Therfield entered the coffee shop confidently, bought a cup of tea at the counter, glanced at those sitting at the tables, then walked over to Scott and eased himself into the seat opposite.

Scott glanced briefly at him, then returned his eyes to the entrance to the Eiffel Hotel.

Miles Therfield was in his early thirties, but his bald head made him appear ten years older. Of medium height, he moved well and clearly was in good condition. He was a sound man who had come into the operational sphere after five years in the Army, two of which were in the SAS. Therfield's attributes were his thoroughness and reliability, his obedience and his occasional initiatives. He would probably never become a top operative, as his innate inclination to follow instructions made him disinclined to operate outside his brief. A top operative must know instinctively when to depart from instructions and go for the unforeseen initiative.

"Book in at the hotel and explain away your lack of luggage. Try for the sixth floor and watch Room 667, having checked that Al Fransen is in there when you take up observation. Arrange with reception that you will leave a note requiring a phone call to be made, as you leave the hotel. Unless you have to follow Fransen out of the hotel, you need not contact the office. If you have to trail Fransen, try to phone me, but don't risk losing him. Any questions?"

" Why are we checking on our friends?"

" He may be acting out of character; I can give you no more guidance right now."

Scott rose and left the coffee shop, standing for a few moments on the corner before seeing Therfield leave and cross the road to the hotel. Five minutes later he saw Therfield at the window of 671 with the telephone in his hand, then he saw him raise both hands in the air. Recognising the signal, he hailed a taxi.

*   *   *

By half-past eleven Scott was sitting in Trewen's room.

" Fransen is in his hotel room at present and I should hear if he leaves there. Primrose is off-duty and Therfield is maintaining watch."

" What did you learn from your contact with Fransen yesterday?"

" Nothing of any value. I took him down to the Compleat Angler at Marlow, yesterday. We had a leisurely lunch and finally I took him back to the hotel at six in the evening. He didn't move from his room, as far as we can tell from our watch outside."

" I'm more concerned to have your view of his state of mind and attitude."

" Although he spoke in a relatively calm manner, I felt he was under some strain. There was a distinct tension throughout our time together and he certainly didn't relax at any time. When I took the conversation away from reminiscence and social chatter, he was clearly concerned that the conversation should not assume a serious nature and he worked hard to preserve the light tone. I tried him on the political scene, but he simply made a joke and side-stepped the need to pursue the subject."

"You made it clear that your interest was purely social, I hope."

"I followed your instructions, but he's very wary and concerned to preserve his freedom of action."

"Your instructions are to be co-operative; do nothing to impede Fransen in any way, but you are to maintain a watch on him, as far as your limited resources permit. As you know, you are relieved of your normal duties during the currency of this surveillance."

"Can you tell me more of Fransen's intentions. Some better idea would help in a situation where our resources are so small."

"There is a possibility that he has some aggressive intention, but we have no basis for any action at present. For the time being, I am concerned to see whether he spends any length of time at a particular place and from this determine whether there is a prospect of him making a move of some sort."

"Our information indicates that he was in the country for twenty-four hours before we began to watch him. In his position, I would have done my checking out immediately on arrival, particularly if my presence were not known to the local station."

"Quite. I think it very likely that is so. However, I want to hear if any move is made by Fransen today. I shall be here until eleven tonight and you are able to reach me subsequently. I also wish you to maintain contact in case any change is necessary in your assignment."

"Certainly. Are there any instructions regarding Floydd?"

"Again, I want no overt action to be taken to impede

Floydd. Do you feel your watch on Fransen would permit Primrose to be detached to watch for Floydd?"

"I will try to. I have the feeling that Primrose would relish the assignment. There was no sign of Floydd at the Eiffel Hotel today, I suppose it would be too much to hope that his interest in Fransen continues and that we may spot him from our watch on Fransen."

"I hope every effort will be made to locate him before nightfall. His clothing is not a disguise and he is likely to be similarly dressed today. It is not my intention to ask any of our other services to assist in locating him; there is no reason to involve them at this juncture. We may decide to bring him in, consequently Primrose should maintain contact with you to the maximum degree. Do impress on Primrose that his instructions could change."

*   *   *

Primrose sounded sleepy and disgruntled when he answered the telephone.

"Are you capable of coming into action immediately? I know you've had only a brief rest, but I think you'd like to have the chance to trace the man you spotted. Come in by taxi right away."

"For a shot at that, I can make it pretty rapidly."

Primrose was keen to have an assignment which might bring him to notice. If he could get hold of Floydd and find out where he had been or evidence that he was the fourth man, his name would certainly be given attention.

He dressed rapidly in the clothes he had taken off only three hours before, grabbed a piece of cheese and watched at the window for the minicab to arrive.

Fifteen minutes later he was in Scott's room.

" You are to concentrate on trying to find Floydd before sundown. He is likely to be dressed in the same way. It seems he may really be down on his luck, or at least committed to using it as a cover. Where you will find him, I can't tell you. Therfield is on watch in the Eiffel Hotel in room 671.

" It's possible Floydd has left central London, but I want you to concentrate there nevertheless."

" Have we alerted the police or the other services and issued descriptions or photographs?"

" No. It's your assignment and you are on your own completely. Keep in touch with the office at intervals of not more than half an hour and let us know the moment you locate him. You are not to interfere with Floydd. We may pull him, but even that isn't certain. Keep in touch so that you know how to act when contact is made."

" What about Fransen?"

Primrose had been kept from the facts on that assignment and his pride demanded that he should learn the significance of the surveillance, particularly since Floydd had been outside Fransen's hotel.

" He's at the hotel; there's no indication of a link with Floydd. We have no reason to assume that they will meet or that they are acting in concert. Now, where will you start and what do you see as your plan?"

" Will you tell me if Fransen leaves the hotel and where he's heading?"

" You'll be told of any significant move, but don't waste time on the phone asking for information. Simply call in and we'll tell you anything you need to know; you need every possible moment on the pavement. Now, what's your plan?"

" I want our vehicle for half an hour. I'll cover the area

70

from the hotel along the Embankment to Vauxhall Bridge, back through Westminster, Piccadilly and the Strand. Then I'll try the loungers along these routes. I should be able to cover the area reasonably well, but there's no certainty of spotting him."

" Fine, go ahead on that basis. One point in addition. If you see Fransen at any time and Therfield or I are not in contact with him, you are to switch to Fransen and let us know as soon as you can, without running the risk of losing him. The instructions on Fransen are to observe, report and not to interfere with his movements."

The prospect of tracking down Floydd, despite the odds against success, had lifted the fatigue he had felt and he left the room determined to do more than locate him. He would get something concrete from Floydd.

TWELVE

The phone call put Fransen on the alert. He doubted that it really had been a check by a male telephone operator to ensure that his extension was functioning correctly. The affability of Scott the previous day and his willingness to spend a good deal of time with him, had given him the impression that he might be under surveillance. Now they were checking that he was in the room, before taking up a closer watch. This suggested a person in close proximity; unless they had obtained the co-operation of the hotel management.

"Give me reception, please."

Fransen noted that the operator he now spoke to was a girl, as had been the case throughout his stay.

"I've just seen someone in the hotel whose face is very familiar to me, but I surely don't want to be embarrassed by coming face to face with him and having to admit that I just don't recall his name. He must have booked into the hotel about half an hour ago and he's probably on my floor. This is Fransen in 667."

"Just one moment, sir. I'll look in the registration cards. It would only be likely to be either Mr. Tranter, who is staying with us with his wife, or Mr. Field who is on your floor in 671. He did ask for a room on the sixth floor, I remember."

"Why that's the guy; you certainly have saved me from putting my foot right in it. Thank you for your help."

Now he knew how close they were and that they were not operating with the assistance of the management. If he went out, he would pass Field's door, unless he used the stairs.

He must take a walk, otherwise they would be concerned by his apparent failure to go out at all. Fransen looked out of the window and found that there was no sign of rain and therefore no need to take a top coat with him. He crossed to the breakfast trolley and left a note on its lower deck, which was covered by the drapes of the damask cloth spread on the top deck.

Fransen left the room, careful not to glance at the door of 671, rang for the lift and descended. He waited in the foyer, determining whether a watch was also being kept there. Satisfied, he nodded to the reception clerk and walked out into the sunlight. He paused again at the corner; he wanted to be sure that his shadow followed him and to identify him.

This would be Field now, he decided, as he saw a man emerge rapidly from the hotel and look in each direction. Fransen moved off and began to walk briskly towards the Strand, turned left and crossed the road, after again satisfying himself that Field was following.

He went on and turned right, seeing the central area of Covent Garden ahead of him. Fransen found it a fascinating place at any hour. The frantic bustle at first light, when lorry loads of fruit and vegetables were sold and now the complete absence of activity, but the area redolent with the lingering smells of the produce and lying abandoned in the gutters, lettuces, tomatoes and grapefruit. The fruit and vegetables in reasonable condition which had been left on the ground had already been removed by the less fortunate. Fransen walked on, arriving at the front of the Opera House and entered between the columns. He obtained a

73

programme for the season and proceeded, looking at the operas and ballets to be performed and the artistes who were to appear.

Back in his room, he was satisfied that undue interest would not be attracted by his apparent failure to emerge from his room during the rest of the day.

It was important that he had everything in perfect order in case that night provided the opportunity for action. In Dallas he had had support, but here he was on his own and he must make sure that no hitch occurred. He opened the small case and rapidly fitted together the parts of the short-stocked collapsible rifle, clipping the infra-red telescopic sight into place. Taking a cartridge, he slipped it into the breech, then ejected it. Then he carefully polished the lenses of the telescopic sight.

He unscrewed the silencer, dismantled the weapon and replaced it in the case. Taking his automatic from his shoulder holster, he checked the action and fitted the silencer. Satisfied that all was in order, he unscrewed the silencer and replaced it in the case, slipping the automatic under a newspaper on the desk.

It was time for lunch and he went over to the telephone. " Room service, please. I should like some *pâté*, followed by a fillet steak, rare, a green salad, cheese and biscuits and iced water. Have it sent up at one o'clock."

Fransen checked the time, picked up his bottle of Scotch and poured himself a measure, adding soda water. He walked over to the window, looking down at the Thames as he drank.

Half an hour later there was a knock at the door. Fransen opened the door, allowing the waiter to wheel in the trolley. Having closed and locked the door he went to the trolley, lifting the cloth.

" You got my note, is everything arranged?"

" No problems, the clothes are there and my mate will come up when he comes off duty at three o'clock. He wants thirty pounds not the twenty he agreed to."

The waiter was doubtful whether Fransen would agree; they might be milking him too hard.

" Look, we agreed on twenty for each of you. I guess you're going to split the extra ten between you."

" Well I could handle it myself, but you said yesterday you didn't always want the same person coming up and you had to have a man with black hair."

He was sure they would get the money now.

" Make sure he's here at three sharp, I don't want any problems."

From under the trolley cloth, Fransen took a short, white waiter's jacket, black trousers and a black bow tie. Going to the bathroom, he slipped them on, satisfying himself that they were a reasonable fit.

Returning to the room, he saw that the waiter had put a chair in front of the trolley, rearranged the cloth and set the cutlery.

" Fits fine. Now make sure he's up here on time, Jack, or the whole deal's off."

" He will be, don't worry, now he knows he's going to get the extra money. His name's Frank Simmons."

" Great, cut along now."

Fransen went back to the bathroom, so that his disguise could not be seen from the corridor when Jack opened the door to leave, then sat down to eat his lunch.

When he finished, he reset his alarm clock for a quarter to three and stretched out on the bed.

He awoke seconds before the alarm was due to go off, rose and washed. He took a light raincoat from the wardrobe, folded it and put it on the lower deck of the trolley, placing the rifle case beside it.

The knock on the door came at three o'clock and he let Frank in. Fransen pulled out six, five pound notes from his bill fold.

" Here's your cash, Frank. Make sure you follow the drill perfectly. Just after I leave, slip your arm round the door and fasten the Do Not Disturb notice to the door knob. Don't answer the phone if it rings and don't answer the door. Got that?"

" Yes, you'll get what you've paid for. I'll wait here till you come back."

Fransen noticed his eyes go to the whisky bottle.

" No drinking while I'm out; you can have an extra fiver if you stay away from it."

Fransen picked up the receiver and told the operator that he wanted no calls, as he had a great deal of work to do and would take a nap when he had completed it. He went into the bathroom, slipped on his shoulder holster and put in the automatic. He put on the waiter's jacket and picked up the black wig, slipping it on with practised ease. He looked himself over, went into the room, nodded to Frank and wheeled the trolley to the door. He tapped the Do Not Disturb notice and Frank nodded in his turn.

He wheeled the trolley along the corridor to the lift. As he waited, a hand emerged from his room to hang the notice on the door knob.

Suddenly he realised that he was being watched from the corridor by Field. With apparent lack of interest, Field turned away as the door of 667 closed; it had been the door not Fransen he had been watching.

The service lift arrived and as planned, it contained Jack. As they descended, he took off the black bow tie and replaced it with an ordinary blue tie. He took out the raincoat and put it on. When they reached the basement, he took the rifle case and left the lift, from which Jack emerged a few seconds later wheeling the trolley.

Fransen ran up the stairs to the ground floor and left the hotel, hailing a taxi a few yards down the road.

*   *   *

As the taxi passed under Admiralty Arch, Fransen leaned forward and told the driver to pull up a few yards down the Mall.

Fransen left the taxi and walked to Horse Guards Road. He slowed to a stroll as he neared the Guards Memorial, stopping from time to time to look up at the buildings. He was already regretting the need to wear the raincoat, which covered the waiter's jacket. The warmth of the sun made it uncomfortably hot.

As his gaze swung to the park, he was intrigued to note the interest of two men, standing well back, in something beyond the monument. He continued walking and as he moved clear of the memorial, he saw a figure which was vaguely familiar, seated on a bench.

The bearded tramp rose and began to limp towards the lake. Fransen was relieved that he had not been recognised and blessed his black wig.

Now that the tramp was well away from the road, Fransen walked on eventually turning into Parliament Square, then going on into Whitehall. He stopped at the corner of Downing Street.

He turned, flagged a taxi and five minutes later walked into the foyer of his hotel. He went over to the internal telephone booth and asked for room service, ordering a

77

prawn cocktail, ham salad and a bottle of whisky to be sent to his room immediately.

The booth phone rang after a few minutes. As arranged, Jack was speaking and confirmed that he was about to take up the trolley.

Shortly afterwards the service lift arrived, the doors opened and Jack was inside. As soon as the doors closed behind him, Fransen removed his raincoat, putting it on the lower deck of the trolley and took off his tie, replacing it with the bow tie. While making these alterations to his appearance, he gave Jack his instructions.

" Come and collect the trolley in half an hour, there'll be more money for you and Frank, so keep him here in the hotel."

At the sixth floor Fransen stepped from the lift, wheeling the trolley and leaving Jack behind. He walked to the room door and knocked diffidently, then took the key from his pocket and let himself in.

He gestured to Frank to remain silent until he had closed the door.

" Go down and wait with Jack, don't leave the building; there's more money if you play this straight. Here's your extra five pounds for staying away from the liquor."

" Anything you say, sir."

Frank took the note and delayed opening the door until Fransen had slipped into the bathroom.

The food did not appeal. What he needed was a drink and he opened the new bottle, forgetting the unfinished one on the tray and poured himself a stiff drink. He carried it into the bathroom, removed the wig and waiter's uniform and drew on his own slacks.

He knocked back the rest of the drink, suddenly realising that the Do Not Disturb sign was still outside. For Field's benefit he showed himself in the doorway when he removed it.

When Jack arrived for the trolley, Fransen had mapped out the scheme and explained to him the part to be played by the two waiters.

THIRTEEN

" The President will watch from the Admiralty."

The Prime Minister stared out of the window at the rose garden, as he spoke. Turning, he waved Trewen to a seat, continuing to stand and glancing at the garden occasionally as they talked. He was interested to be briefed on the position regarding Fransen, but clearly was preoccupied with digesting the content of his discussion with the President.

He had convinced himself that the divisive issues which separated the two countries were largely the product of the President's determination to create an impregnable position for himself and his party in the forthcoming presidential elections. He was sure of the Democratic nomination, but not certain he would be the people's choice. They had rejected him after he had served out the remainder of Kennedy's term. He had secured the Democratic nomination in the 1964 election, but been badly beaten by the hard line Republican candidate. Retaining leadership of his party in the following period had been an intolerable burden, but he had managed it, only to be narrowly beaten by the incumbent in the following election.

Having fought so long and hard to become president in his own right, he was determined to have his second permitted term, no matter what it cost. He had called his strategists together a year before, to determine the issues most likely to influence the outcome of the election and to plot the course for the twelve months which followed, so that in the succeeding, run-up year to the election he would have an effective platform.

The President had been perturbed when his advisers spelt out the need to go against the interests of his allies, in order to placate the Russians and the Chinese. That would facilitate a reduction in the defence budget, providing funds for a medical care programme and permitting lower taxation levels, which together would guarantee his second term.

The Prime Minister had tried to demonstrate to the President that, in making up for the American defence deficiency, the increased British expenditure would bring down the nation's economy. He sought to convince the President that his measures to protect American industry, at the expense of British and European exports, would bring the whole of the West to a total economic impasse, which would be reflected in their ability to resist Communist pressures in their own countries, ultimately increasing America's vulnerability.

His line of argument had failed to impress the President and he had achieved no concessions, having to accept a promise to review the proposals, which he knew to be a diplomatic fiction.

Only in persuading the President to watch the ceremony from an Admiralty window had he achieved any success. It was a strange paradox that his sole achievement was the protection from a possible assassin of a man who was pursuing policies more harmful to Britain than those of any politician since Stalin.

The Prime Minister became conscious that he had stood for some time saying nothing, but he had now made his decision.

" The interests of the President have been safeguarded by my action. You will take no action against Fransen, unless he acts in a manner contrary to the laws of this country."

Trewen realized that this left a massive gap, but knew it was pointless to probe it.

" Did the CIA appear to be inclined to trade information, when you told them about Floydd?"

" They offered nothing. Fransen's name was mentioned by them in relation to Floydd, but nothing more. I am reasonably satisfied that they are not controlling him and could be unaware of his presence in this country. On Floydd they were interested, but their resources are stretched at the moment and I doubt that they have the men to divert to seeking him out."

" Have you anything which provides substantive proof that an attempt will be made to assassinate the President? Has anything happened which provides evidence of an attempt by Fransen or anyone else?"

" We have no further information and no firm evidence, but I feel we would be wise to place some credence on the warning given by Floydd."

" Floydd, surely his name was Clive? He may be acting against Fransen and that is adequately balanced by the possible interference in his actions by the CIA. We shall be able to demonstrate a concern for the President's safety and a desire to co-operate. Should a rogue CIA man break from the herd and cause a regrettable accident, the fault cannot be laid at our door. Indeed, the fact that he chose to act in this country suggests nothing more than a reprehensible desire to implicate us."

" It could be suggested that this represented another weakness in our security network."

" Nonsense. We cannot control CIA men. This is not a security matter, concerning nuclear weapons or defence secrets. If Fransen were to attack the President, it would be a question of one of their intelligence men acting in accordance with his own conscience against a leader who could be taking his country into an intolerable position."

The Prime Minister's peroration was well under way and he took advantage of a momentary pause to rise in the hope of escaping.

" I wish to ensure that all is in order."

" Certainly, Charles. And please remember that your present information provides no evidence that an attempt will be made on the President's life, by Fransen or anyone else."

He turned again to the rose garden, failing to respond to Trewen's farewell.

The paper they were preparing on the Vice-President would be interesting. He was looking forward to reading it.

Concern for the stability and defence of his country and his disdain for the self-seeking policies of the President had now overcome the moral attitudes which he had professed, in the years before and immediately subsequent to his entry into Parliament.

FOURTEEN

Seldom in his career had Trewen been involved in a situation as distasteful and complex as that which now confronted him. His natural inclination was to act to preserve the life of the American head of state, but little could be done without upsetting the relationship with the CIA, if the likely assassin was a member of that organisation.

Trewen asked his secretary to check whether Emnie could spare him a few minutes. Their wives would arrive for the ceremony later and in the interim he felt that his anxiety would be eased by a chat with Emnie, to whom he might choose to talk with some freedom.

*   *   *

" Come in and have a chair. Anne and Diana won't be here for some time, but I felt we might have a word together. Have you heard further from Floydd?"

" Nothing. No further contact, Charles. Was it possible to avoid identifying him as your source?"

" No, I was forced to reveal the source and in any event CS already knew he was back in play. It may well be that he is brought in for us to talk to him."

" That would be a great pity. I only hope he moved on as I suggested to him. He behaved in a creditable way in contacting me and it would be a shame if the consequence

84

was to be his loss of freedom and the peace of mind he gave up so much to find."

" All that is perfectly true, but we all know that we can never opt out of this work. Some factor can always arise which could lead to our reinvolvement. Clive Floydd could not resist the compulsion to warn us, so that an aggressive act could be frustrated, not that there is any positive indication that Fransen has any such intention."

The conversation was not taking the course he had anticipated and far from easing his anxiety by a frank interchange, he was becoming increasingly concerned that Emnie felt himself personally involved. This was uncharacteristic and he had to prevent the inclination from developing.

" Roger, it is essential that you put out of your mind the suggestion which Floydd made to you. The whole matter is in hand and the responsibility now lies elsewhere. You know only too well the need for you to relinquish your interest on passing over a matter of this type."

Emnie looked at him steadily. Several interpretations were possible. Clearly Trewen had some specific course in mind which might concern him, otherwise such a comment would have been unnecessary between senior colleagues. His speculation on Trewen's intentions was interrupted by Trewen rising.

" Shall we go down to the control room and see what is going on? You'll be pleased to know that the President has been persuaded to watch the parade from the Admiralty and not from the saluting base."

" I'm glad to hear it. If Floydd's brought in for questioning, he may find it some consolation that his warning had some effect, even though it's hardly a fair exchange."

*　　*　　*

85

In the control room it was possible to monitor police information on the situation in the area around Westminster, Whitehall and the West End of London. Information of significance to the ceremony was being collated in one section and to the police information was added intelligence from the security services and the armed forces on duty in the area.

Trewen asked for a situation report, found nothing of significance and turned to find Emnie was no longer beside him. He crossed the room and joined Emnie, who stood beside an array of television monitors, with pictures from cameras mounted on buildings to observe activity in critical areas of the capital.

Crowds had not yet built up, but some spectators were beginning to straggle towards Horse Guards Parade. Emnie immediately turned and Trewen accompanied him to the door, a little surprised that he had not asked whether anything of interest had come in.

In the corridor Emnie hesitated.

" I really must go back to my office. I should be able to join you by the time our wives get here."

" Certainly, I'll give them a drink and look after them until you join us. Sorry that I pulled you away, but I wanted to have this chat with you."

" Not at all, I was very pleased to hear of the President's change of plan. I hope to be clear of it all well before the ceremony starts and I should certainly be able to have a drink with you. Give Diana my love and apologise to them both, if I don't clear things as rapidly as I would hope."

Trewen watched Emnie set off briskly down the corridor; he was clearly more tense than he had been earlier. On his return to his room, Trewen was delighted to find his secretary had produced a tray of sandwiches and coffee.

As he poured the coffee, she placed decanters of whisky and brandy beside the glasses and went to fetch water and a soda syphon.

Half an hour later, his secretary told him she was going down to collect his wife and Anne Emnie.

The wives came into the room. They had dined together and were in a suitably relaxed mood to enjoy the spectacle from a privileged position.

Having exchanged greetings, both accepted brandy.

" Roger has something urgent to handle, but he hopes to be clear by the time we go down to watch from the conference room."

Anne Emnie sat watchful and serious as ever. Her dress was long and on someone else could have been elegant, her black hair well groomed, but a shade too coarse for his liking. Her sharp face correctly suggested that she was a woman of considerable intellect.

Diana Trewen in contrast was totally relaxed and very much at ease. She was elegant without being beautiful; a handsome woman, whose clothes and auburn hair added to her charm. Her brain was not as acute as Anne's, but her judgement of people was perceptive.

*   *   *

They had finally decided to go down to the conference room without Emnie and stood looking down on Horse Guards Parade. The crowd on either side of the memorial was already three deep behind the metal barriers and a third of the reserved seats in the stands were occupied.

" I fear that Roger has become more involved than he had intended. Let's sit down; Beating Retreat takes over an hour when the Guards Division is on parade."

As they watched, the empty spaces filled rapidly and the standing room seemed glutted. Diana looked over at the building opposite.

" Even the windows of the Admiralty seem fully committed tonight."

Trewen followed his wife's remark by examining the windows, noting one occupied by only one man. Its excellent position suggested that the President and his party would come forward to occupy it later.

He gestured as he saw a movement in the shadows.

" You can see the trumpeters moving into position on top of the Admiralty command centre."

The figures of the State Trumpeters of the Household Cavalry moved into position, standing in a well spaced line.

The lights dimmed; it was half-past nine and the chimes of Big Ben rang out clearly on the air. The heat of the day was gone and a light breeze fanned the faces of those waiting for the ceremony to commence. The last glimmers of light from the setting sun were gone.

As the final note from Big Ben sounded, the trumpeters raised their instruments, illuminated by the floodlights suddenly directed on them.

FIFTEEN

Emnie went to the cupboard which formed part of the bookcase and took out a bottle of whisky and a glass. He poured a large measure, replaced the bottle and went across the room to sit at his desk. There were more comfortable chairs to sit in, but he preferred to concentrate his mind by sitting in a firm chair, with a pencil and paper before him.

He raised the glass and drank half its contents. He was not a hardened drinker; he seldom drank straight alcohol before dinner and a spasm marked his face, recording his reaction, not his distaste. The whisky hit his stomach and he felt better.

Emnie was virtually certain that in the control room Trewen's attention to the situation report had prevented his looking at the monitors and seeing the lone figure. He hoped his departure had not alerted Trewen.

From his internal telephone guide he checked the numbers of the Night Duty office and the Security Officer.

" Duty Officer here."

Emnie recognized the voice.

" Evening, Henry, Emnie here. I require immediately a packet of one hundred pounds in single used notes. Please send it down immediately, in a sealed envelope with a receipt, by messenger."

" Certainly, Mr. Emnie."

He drank a smaller quantity of whisky and dialled the

number of the Security Officer.

"I shall be out for about half an hour and I shall require a secure room on my return. Please ensure that it has a table, two chairs and a camp bed with blankets. Arrange for some coffee and sandwiches also. I anticipate returning with somebody, so please instruct the security guard on duty suitably.

"Certainly, Mr. Emnie. I should be able to arrange all that within thirty minutes. I presume the room will be required overnight."

"Plan for twenty-four hours at present and, thank you."

"I'll speak to the guard on duty immediately and I will be available on your return. Goodbye, Mr. Emnie."

Emnie finished his drink and went over to the bookcase and put away the empty glass, turning as there was a knock at the door. He was sufficiently on edge to go over to the door and open it himself.

To his relief he found that it was the messenger with a bulky envelope. He took it, opening it with his finger as he walked to the desk. He extracted a bundle of used pound notes, with a paper band round them. It was about the correct thickness, so he took the receipt and signed it. He thanked the messenger, who left as he squeezed the notes into his jacket pocket.

Having locked his room, he went rapidly to the staircase and went down. The guard on the door had clearly been told to expect him.

"I shall watch for you in about half an hour, Mr. Emnie."

The guard's eyes went to the envelope which protruded from his pocket and he opened the doors leading to Whitehall.

"Please do watch for me; I shall wish to enter without

delay."

Emnie stepped out into the street, at Downing Street he paused, having intended to go into it, but realised that tickets were being checked at the far end. He had no ticket for the ceremony and to establish his status would take time.

He decided to continue down Whitehall as far as King Charles Street and turned into it, surprised to see some vacant car parking spaces there, despite the number of cars searching for space on Whitehall and the roads opposite. He hurried along the short road and turned right, into Horse Guards Road, being forced to slow by the volume of sightseers who were moving up the road. He crossed over and entered the park, heading for the Guards Memorial and towards the pile of wooden hurdles. He reached the spot twenty yards back from the road, where he had seen the overcoated figure on the monitor, but there was no sign of him.

Emnie walked in each direction, trying to catch some glimpse of the limping figure, but he could not see Floydd. The chimes of Big Ben for half-past eight made him realise that the light would soon be gone; the noise level was high and the volume of people was increasing steadily.

No police were in sight and those in the park were moving towards him and the ceremony. If he did not find him rapidly, the task would be impossible and he would have to consider whether to report this sighting.

As he passed a bench, he heard a phrase from the conversation of an eldrly pair of women sitting there.

" Can't think what they were fighting for. . . ."

Emnie hesitated, realizing that he nothing else to go on.

" Did you see some sort of scuffle here in the past few minutes?"

" Yes, well, no. It must have been about half an hour ago."

The second woman interrupted her friend.

" There was three of them and only two came back a few minutes ago."

She succeeded in injecting considerable drama into the words, but she was interrupted in her turn.

" They almost dragged him away."

Emnie realised that he could listen to the duet for some time without adding materially to his knowledge and interjected.

" Where did they take him?"

" Over there."

Emnie hurried away in the direction they had pointed, neglecting to thank them. He went across the neck of land, onto the peninsula, which only just fails to be an island. He moved through some undergrowth in trying to reach the water's edge, then stood still, hoping to be guided by some sound or movement, some sign that he had not reached Floydd too late.

The only movement he could detect appeared to result from his having disturbed some moorhens. Then he noticed some down-trodden undergrowth and moved in that direction. He suddenly picked up the smell of whisky and went over to a tree.

There Floydd lolled, his back supported by the tree, his head sunk on his chest, overcoat unbuttoned, arms open, legs splayed. Near his feet lay a flat half bottle of whisky, virtually empty. From the strength of the whisky aroma, it was obvious that the ground as well as Floydd's clothes had been liberally doused with the contents of the bottle. Emnie stood looking down at Floydd.

Time no longer mattered. The passage of ten seconds or

ten minutes was unimportant, as he looked at him propped against the tree, defenceless.

He knew that he had done this to a man he had valued and respected.

Emnie knew he was not a man of action, but at that moment he swore he would find out who had done this. He would find them and make sure they paid for the way Floydd had been killed. He might not take part in the final act against them, but he would ensure it occurred.

As he bent down he knew Floydd was dead, the smell of whisky, which had comforted him so recently, sickened him and that seemed one more despicable act. They had tried to pass off Floydd as a drunken vagrant.

Only as his face neared Floydd's did he realise how disfigured he was; someone had hit him hard and often. Emnie looked again at his right arm and appreciated that it was not simply open at his side, but lying at a strange angle, broken.

SIXTEEN

By nine o'clock it was almost impossible to pass along the pavement on the open side of Horse Guards Parade. The crowds were held in check at the front by the metal barriers and the way kept clear for the entry in thirty minutes of the bands taking part.

Some good humour was being shown and help given to the children, so that they might watch from the front. Generally, however, the main interest was that each person should retain their position of vantage.

The crowd was seven deep in places and some children had climbed onto the pile of hurdles, enjoying a good view over the heads of the adults.

As the quarter struck, the trumpeters took their places on the Admiralty command centre and another eight moved onto the top of the Palace of Westminster. The gates beneath were closed. No further people would be admitted other than the official party to be seated at the saluting base.

It was twilight, the last glimmer of light almost gone. Men stood beside the searchlights placed on the stands, but no light was visible from them. All illumination, other than that from the park, had been extinguished and the crowd became silent, suddenly conscious of the noise of the generators, which would power the searchlights.

As the light finally faded, the half-hour tolled out from Big Ben and, as the last note died, the searchlights spotlighted the sixteen State trumpeters, as they raised their long ceremonial trumpets to their lips.

In perfect unison each began to blow the opening notes of the Last Post. Each matched the others note for note, the light reflected by the breastplates and the helmets, beneath the white plumes of the Life Guards and the red plumes of the Blues, Royal Horse Guards and 1st Dragoons.

The last sad note ended and the floodlights were cut. The horses, which they had heard positioned, were not moving forward, they stood, occasional hooves pawing the road surface. The searchlights flashed on and focussed on the mounted bands of the Household Cavalry, as they moved forward, swinging in two lines onto the parade ground. As the lights moved forward with the mounted bands, the saluting base was illuminated for the first time and the eight seated figures were obvious.

The crowd strained to identify the figures.

*　　*　　*

From a window of the Admiralty, the President looked down at the pageant beneath him, conscious that no military parade in his country could match this splendour. Regretting the lack for an instant, before he reminded himself that his nation's strength had been built on the desire and ability to look forward and not back.

The lights had again been lowered and the hesitant first notes of the bagpipes were heard, the floodlights picking out the pipers of the Scots and Irish Guards. The massed drums followed and their insistent rhythm brought home the great military strength of the musical partnership. The pipes alone could bring gaiety and sadness, but with the drums they produced a measure to add to the courage of any man.

Having countermarched, two circles were formed by the pipers and their sad chant went forth, changing as the drumming entered again, becoming more vital, until the drums ceased and the pipes, full of their boundless hope, faded and the lights went down again.

It was colder now, the breeze quite perceptible, heat being drawn from the surrounding buildings, stored from the sunshine of the day. Had anyone looked up, they would have seen the stars shining brightly, but the effect of the floodlights was to produce the impression of total darkness, in the minutes which passed while the next section of the bands formed up.

They saw the massed corps of drums march on, their fifes and drums overcoming their tonal limitations and, with their insistent rhythm, showing how they had inspired those who had marched behind in a thousand campaigns. Here the President agreed; it was a common musical facet of the military heritage of both nations.

Before the final ensemble, when each section of the bands joined with the others, came the marching and counter-marching of the bands of the Foot Guards, changing at one point from a rousing quick march to a superb arrangement of a Beatles hit.

The whole performance was drawing to an end. Any attempt on the President at his window, or on those on the saluting base, would have to be made now and Trewen found his attention was no longer on the splendour, the colour and music below him. The attempt must come in the next few minutes and, if from the park, the apprehension of the assassin would be well-nigh impossible unless he was immobilized by the crowd. From what he had learned of Fransen, Trewen felt he would make the attack even if his escape was uncertain and that his operational skill would optimise any chance of liberty. Scott would be able to do little until it was too late, if he followed his instructions, always assuming he had been able to maintain contact.

Again Trewen mused on his own responsibility in the whole affair. He recognised the need to regard the safety of one's country as being above the dictates of one's conscience, but he had been stunned by the mild-mannered, old man's decision.

How could a schoolmaster, a man with immense charisma among union men, valued as a man who cared about their condition and their future, have inured himself in his period in office to make such a totally uncharacteristic decision. A man of high principle, who had to adapt his thinking in order to meet the small-minded demands of practical politics, had been Trewen's assessment.

Now he was aware of his total failure to understand the old man.

What he had taken for the character of the man was the smooth exterior of the skilled politician, who had devoted his whole life to the acquisition of power.

SEVENTEEN

Emnie put his hand into Floydd's beard immediately in front of the right ear. This represented only a final superfluous confirmation that he was dead.

To his amazement, he felt a tiny, thready pulse, so faint that he wondered whether it was only his imagination. He knelt beside Floydd and raised his right eyelid. The pupil was dilated, indicating cerebral damage. He wondered what he could do to stimulate Floydd; to touch or disturb his head would be madness. Feeling that he was doing something ineffectual; no more than was done in romantic novels for fainting heroines, he chafed Floydd's remaining good hand.

The eyelids fluttered, the lips drew back, blood oozed from between them and Emnie saw the stumps of two teeth and a number of gaps. Floydd had taken a terrible beating to the head and elsewhere, judging by the broken arm. His breathing became a series of gasps which seemed to Emnie to come from the depths of his lungs and this convinced him that Floydd had taken a number of kicks or punches to the chest and body.

Floydd's eyes moved slowly from left to right, passing over Emnie, without focussing or taking him in.

" Clive, what happened."

The eyes wandered, then with a visible effort, Floydd moved his head and his eyes showed some recognition. The face was too badly beaten to show any signs of Floydd's feelings as he spoke and his mouth too damaged for any hint to come to Emnie from his voice.

" You did this to me. You finished me."

Blood spattered from his lips as he spoke. His eyes were hard and Emnie found himself watching Floydd's mouth, unsure whether he was avoiding his eyes, or simply trying to concentrate harder on the indistinct words.

" I've just arrived here."

Emnie was sure now that Floydd's mind had gone and that he was attributing his misfortune to the first face he saw on recovering consciousness.

" They didn't find me by chance. They talked after they thought I was unconscious, when he'd beaten and kicked me and before his chum gave me the injection."

" Can I do anything?"

" No. Nothing. I know I'm finished. My clean life recently must have given me more resistance than they anticipated. You must have laughed when I phoned you this morning. Fancy contacting the fourth man, who could bring down any group against me. Now your cover's perfect, you'll be able to sling mud at me and fake evidence with your friends to show I was linked with Philby. You'll have difficulty proving I was involved in the killing of the President, but maybe you can manage that too. Is it that you hate me, or have we always been on different sides? As he savaged me, your chum muttered that he had been told to make it tough when the time came."

As he spoke, Floydd's words became clearer and he seemed to gain in concentration.

" I had nothing to do with it, Clive. I had to tell Trewen my source and you'd already been spotted by CS, which made it easy for him to deduce my source."

99

"They said they tracked me from a tip, tracked me for hours. Only you knew we were meeting and could have provided the opportunity of a positive identification of me."

He stopped, weak from the effort and lolled, his breathing short and shallow, his eyes moving from side to side, as he sought the strength and concentration to continue.

Emnie waited. To talk while Floydd fought for the means to prolong his life would be fruitless and seemed to him to be indecent. He found he had little to say other than to deny the accusation. Floydd knew something he had not told him and it was vital to his conviction of Emnie's guilt.

Floydd's condition gave Emnie no hope that he could save him if he went off to obtain help. It might take fifteen minutes or more to get an ambulance and Emnie doubted whether even immediate treatment would measurably increase Floydd's span.

At that moment, with Floydd fighting to control himself and wrench for himself a few more moments of life, the sad notes of the Last Post sounded.

In the Last Post the principal trumpet calls of the day are echoed. The whole life of a day passes from Reveille, through the events to its ending. A whole life in a trumpet call. And now the calm, sad notes were a conclusion.

Floydd seemed to draw strength from the final notes; he knew he was going to die and he was determined to say these last words, to slam home to this despicable sham the enormity of what he had done. It did not amount to a task of great value, but Floydd could not let go, relax and die until he had forced Emnie to face his treachery.

The futility of it all swept over him for an instant and his eyes closed. Then he made his effort, the lids opened, the eyes found Emnie again, the mind fought to focus and to cause the words to be articulated.

"You sat at Junction and watched us all and fed the information to Moscow. You knew, just as well as Philby, the facts they wanted to know. Probably you were recruited by the same man; You could even have been his control . . . but that would have been pointless . . . You had access to a far greater variety of information than Philby and you put them onto me, when I phoned you this morning."

Floydd's voice faded at the end of the accusation.

"You must know that's not true. I've never acted against you and I'm no more guilty of helping Philby than you or anyone else. What I want to know is what happened and who did this."

Floydd grasped the first subject and brought his mind to bear on that rather than the more important question. The need to hurt Emnie had been exhausted by his earlier outburst.

"I'd checked out the best vantage points from which to watch. There was no point in trying to follow Fransen; he would get there despite anything I could do. You've made certain now that I can't act against him. Your people may not have planned the assassination, but you're prepared to take advantage of the chaos it creates and to do everything you can to have Fransen escape."

Floydd looked at Emnie, pausing before continuing. Emnie lowered his head, knowing he could not find words which would convince Floydd of his innocence.

"I spotted a pile of hurdles and decided to watch from there. There was nothing I could do to prevent it, but I had to know what happened, before I dropped out of sight again. I didn't see anyone watching me.

"I knew remaining in one spot for too long could draw attention to me, as I didn't intend getting up on the hurdles until the last moment. I was walking back to the lake when they hit me. They slammed into me hard, to soften me up, then got me over here where they could work undisturbed. He did all the damage he could before he got down to the questions."

Floydd stopped, his eyes closed, his head on his chest. Kneeling beside him, Emnie willed him to continue, to tell him some vital fact. There was no point in interrupting. The best way to find out was to let Floydd talk the whole thing through. Again Floydd's eyes opened and he fixed them on Emnie, finding this a help in forcing his mind to the recent events.

" He kept on asking where I'd been, who'd arranged my departure and what I'd been able to tell my friends. I told the truth, but that was too simple to satisfy them. I suppose it has hurt the vanity of all of you that I could disappear so completely and be able to keep my location secret."

Again the pause, longer now and the fluttering of the eyelids before his eyes opened fully again and the fight to focus and comprehend.

This time it did not work. The eyes simply stared ahead, the breathing brief and shallow.

Emnie realized that he must now interject, otherwise he would learn no more; Floydd needed the stimulus of a question if he was to speak again.

" Who, Clive. Who did it? Tell me who did it. For heaven's sake concentrate and tell me who did this to you."

Emnie stopped as the eyes swung round; hard, dilated, hating what they saw.

" You did it."

It was only a whisper. He paused, summoned up his energy, then stammered out a final almost inaudible whisper.

" You and your wretched flower."

The body convulsed, for a moment Floydd appeared to grow taller, then the body relaxed totally, the head fell onto his chest, the eyes open. Emnie was conscious of the stench of urine mingling with the smell of whisky, as the muscles relaxed releasing the body fluids.

The strains of a lament played by the bagpipes came to his ears as he knelt. A lament, a sorrowing, without hope.

Clive Floydd was dead and he could only guess who had done it.

EIGHTEEN

The fifes and drums had been playing for some time before he became aware of them. He still knelt, staring at Floydd.

As he became conscious of his surroundings, Emnie was aware of rustlings. Prior to finding Floydd, he would have assumed them to be the nocturnal stirrings of the water fowl, rodents or owls. Now he realised that there was no reason to assume Floydd's killers had gone. They might have waited to see whether Floydd was discovered and observed that he had spoken with Emnie. Floydd's final barely audible words had left Emnie as uncertain of them as he was of their meaning, but anyone some distance away could have imagined that the last words had revealed their identity.

The lights illuminating the lake did not shine directly on him and he was largely hidden by the trees and undergrowth, but they made any movement by him perceptible. The killers could be watching the small neck of land joining the promontory to the park.

Emnie rose with difficulty. He had knelt on the hard ground for long enough for his joints to ache and his knees cracked as he straightened up. He stood wondering whether he should do something about Floydd's body.

Although dazed by the events, he appreciated that it might give him some advantage if he did not mention Floydd's death. Indeed, it was important that for the time being the identity of Floydd and his death should be known only to those who had encompassed it.

Emnie began to unbutton the jacket and realised that the dead eyes were staring at his hands. In two movements he closed them.

He wished to be quick and to leave the body as little disturbed as possible, so he confined his search to the inner pocket of the jacket and its two side pockets. He found a variety of papers and since he could not see to read them, stuffed them into his own jacket for examination later.

He straightened up and listened carefully, allowing his eyes to become thoroughly adjusted to the light level and the landscape ahead. He moved forward gently, listening after taking each span of steps. Finally he reached the park again and seeing no one overtly watching him, looked over to the crowd, intent on seeing the countermarching of the fifes and drums.

If he returned directly to the Cabinet Office, he would possibly have little time in which to think, as Trewen might well call him on the intercom. Besides, the orderliness of his office did not appeal and despite the inherent danger, the park seemed more conducive to thought. He set off towards the bridge over the lake, beside which he could sit with some space around him, permitting him to be aware of anyone approaching.

The stars shone down from a clear sky and the moon stood high, the water ruffled slightly by the breeze, the leaves rustling gently on the trees.

Emnie tried to fathom Clive Floydd's final comment, but he found no ready explanation, beginning to doubt whether he had heard the whispered words correctly.

Suddenly he had it. Floydd linked him with CS and Primrose was the flower. He had done it. Long before, there had been a question of his free-lance work connecting him with another security organization.

Emnie began to walk back slowly through the park to Whitehall and as he neared the crowd, he saw from the old palace clock that it was already twenty minutes past ten. He wanted to be back in his room before the end of the ceremony; he must minimise his absence. Emnie walked faster and heard the massed bands playing with the pipes and drums. The programme was nearing its end and he might not now reach his office before the final notes.

He assumed no attempt had been made on the President. All his thinking had been directed to the earliest occasion on which the President would be on view. He had not had time to check the functions which he would attend during the visit. The danger of which Floydd had warned them had not been eliminated by the absence of an attempt by Fransen that night.

The safety of the American head of state was not his proper concern and his continued preoccupation with it was not capable of being sustained through official channels. He had passed over his information to Trewen and that should be an end of it. However the death of Floydd suggested that the problem was not being handled effectively and that the President was still at risk.

Above all, Emnie was determined to follow through in some way himself. He had resolved that those who had killed Floydd should be tracked down and punished.

*   *   *

Emnie left the park elbowing his way through the crowd and crossed the road, having decided to take the direct route through Downing Street, as time was vital to him and there would be no check on those returning by that route.

As he reached the other side of the road, he was met by a shattering roar. Sparks flew in the night air and the sound of the music was overcome.

The emergency field generators, powering the searchlights which were floodlighting the ceremony, were stationed below the steps leading up to Downing Street. The pulsing cacophony of their engines caused the bodies of the generators to oscillate on the springs of the trailers. The exhausts were mounted high in the air and belched their hot breath, interspersed with red sparks, like a quartet of well-drilled dragons, perfectly in line, each contributing an equal share of noise, vibration and pyrotechnics.

Emnie passed them and ran up the steps, dimly hearing the strains of the National Anthem. Clearly there was no time to go to his office and he must go directly to the conference room. He was admitted by the security guard and he asked him to inform the Security Officer that the room would not be required. The reminder of his preparations made him pat his pocket, from which protruded the bulky money-filled envelope.

Both pockets of his jacket bulged as he entered the conference room, his other pocket filled with the papers he had taken from Floydd's jacket.

Anne and Diana and Charles Trewen were turning from the windows as the bands marched off.

" I'm sorry for having been unable to watch with you. Do forgive me, Diana."

He took her hand as he spoke in a graceful gesture at odds with his inelegant appearance. He kissed his wife on the cheek.

" I hope you had a good view and enjoyed it, Anne. I'm sure Charles was an excellent host, but something had to be cleared up and another matter arose while I was in the office."

He looked up at Trewen to gauge whether he had phoned his office and knew he was not there.

" Charles looked after us superbly. I've had a delightful evening. The parade could not have been finer and we had a marvellous view without being exposed to the evening chill. Thank you so much, Charles."

" It was a great pleasure to have you here. I enjoyed it immensely myself and had you and Diana not been here, I would certainly not have bothered to stay on and watch. You become so used to these events arising each year that you forget how splendid they can be."

Trewen was at his most urbane and gracious, but Emnie knew that this was no guarantee he was not curious about his absence. Diana filled a momentary gap in the conversation.

" We shall expect you both for dinner on the seventeenth of next month. I've checked the date with Anne. Dinner was delightful, Anne, thank you again and I'm sorry you missed it all, Roger. I'm sure they would have managed without you if you hadn't been right here, but at least it's a problem you won't have to deal with in the morning."

*　　　*　　　*

They decided not to share a taxi, as Trewen was going up to his room before leaving. Their farewells made, Anne and Roger Emnie went out into Whitehall and were fortunate in finding a taxi immediately.

" It really was rather awkward, your not even being there when we arrived and only coming in when it was all over. It was quite interesting to see, but I gather the President did not attend after all."

" I'm sorry to have missed it and to have caused you embarrassment."

His relationship with Anne had been less than good throughout their marriage and, as so often in the past years, they fell back on formal comments.

They had met when paired at dinner one evening, at a house where he did not know his hosts terribly well. They had a common interest in opera and Anne and he had met at two performances at Covent Garden soon afterwards and this led to an invitation for her to join him on a third occasion.

Emnie's pleasure in their common interest and some indication of attraction to him on her part had led to a fairly rapid marriage, which had proved to be fulfilling for neither of them.

They still had their love of opera, but nothing further had emerged to bring them into a stronger relationship. It seemed that they had discovered their major congruence and what had appeared to be an indication of other possible mutual interests, on which a lasting relationship could be built, turned out to be an isolated, common intellectual pursuit. Their physical relationship had diminished and while they shared the same bed, this seldom led to anything.

Anne did not show any strong indication of frustration in finding their marriage so sterile, but this did not prevent an occasional outburst, which served to bring home to Emnie how little pleasure and contentment they had achieved.

On several occasions he had suggested that they should sleep in separate beds or even separate rooms. This was always rejected by Anne and in doing so she invariably showed unusual tact. It had occurred to Emnie that possibly she had some deep psychological attachment to the double bed as a symbol of her marriage, without which she would feel insecure and threatened. Knowing her deep intellectual strength, he found it hard to convince himself of this; that and the complete absence of reliance on others which she demonstrated in so many ways.

Emnie was convinced that his nightmares and insomnia inevitably affected Anne's rest and he found that on awakening after a vivid dream, at a time when the pressure of his work was high, he would be certain that Anne was awake, even though she preferred to make it appear otherwise.

Emnie was silent as the taxi made its way along Knightsbridge. Then he pretended to remember that he had taken his car in that morning, contrary to his usual practice, because of the phone call from Floydd.

He convinced his wife that it was sensible for him to go back for the car and left her to continue the journey home, warning her that he felt like a walk and would not be back for some time, asking her to go to bed and not wait up for him.

Emnie was able to wave down another taxi and was soon seated in his own car, making his way towards Putney Bridge.

When engaged in an important operation, CS sometimes avoided the need for their operatives to return to their homes and made use of a flat in Putney. If Primrose had killed Floydd, he might decide to spend the night at the flat. He was going to the only address available to him if he wished to reach Primrose before next day.

NINETEEN

Emnie sat in the car for some time outside the flat. It was already half-past eleven. He knew he had no status in the affair, but he had to make sure that the guilt for Floydd's death was established and punishment received.

Finally he decided to go up to the flat and entered the block, which had no porter on duty. He avoided the lift and walked up the sixteen flights of stairs to the eighth floor. Part way up he realised how foolish he was; his heart was beating hard and he felt faint. He could so easily have taken the lift to the seventh floor and walked the rest, if a quiet arrival were so vital.

He stood outside the door of the flat, breathing deeply and trying to ease the constriction in his chest. Having got himself under control, he listened for any sound from the adjoining flats. He knew that he would hear nothing from the CS flat, as it would have a sound attenuating door. The front door fitted perfectly, giving no sign of there being a light on inside.

Emnie rang the bell; had there been a letter box, he might have peered through it, but there was none, letters were deposited in the row of metal boxes in the foyer of the block. He rang the bell a number of times, without response and without the satisfaction of hearing it ring. He decided to resume his search in the morning and rang for the lift.

As he travelled down, it occurred to him that the flat

might no longer be used by CS. On reaching the ground floor, he went over to see the name on the mail box for the flat. The name Rausome on it told him nothing and he crossed the hall to the glass doors.

As he reached for the handle of a door, it swung inward and he was faced by Max Scott. The lighting was poor and Scott had not seen him as he entered.

" Good evening, Mr. Emnie."

Scott recovered first from the surprise of finding Emnie there, not having known that he was aware of the location of the CS flat.

" I'm glad to have run into you."

" It is important, I take it."

Emnie nodded and Scott waved to the lift.

" We'd better talk in the flat."

Neither spoke in the lift, nor until they were in the lounge of the flat. Since Scott was in need of a drink, he suggested that Emnie join him. Emnie looked round the flat as Scott took out a bottle of whisky and glasses.

The couch and arm chairs were worn and of only a moderate quality; the deep maroon of the moquette did nothing to improve the decor of fawn wallpaper and a mid green carpet, distinctly scuffed in front of the chairs and couch. The green floral curtains were closed by Scott before he brought their drinks to the easy chairs, in which they seated themselves opposite one another.

" Do you know where Clive Floydd is? I provided information which confirmed his presence in London today and I am aware of your having sighted him through Primrose."

" I can't tell you any more than you know already, Mr. Emnie. I've not heard anything further on his movements today."

Scott found Emnie's behaviour puzzling and saw no

reason to refuse to discuss the matter, when all he had was a series of telephone messages indicating that Primrose had not located Floydd.

" What is your reason for being interested in this matter, Mr. Emnie?"

" Clive Floydd was a friend of mine. I was the person he contacted and I wished to know whether further contact had been made."

" You mean he is no longer a friend of yours; I notice that you use the past tense."

Emnie tasted his drink for the first time. He should not have asked for the whisky unadulterated, it made him feel sick. He realized that it would give the impression he was trying to put off answering the question, but knew he could not drink it as it was.

" Might I have some soda after all."

He waited until Scott had handed back the glass before replying.

" I have good reason to believe he is dead. My discussion with him today and the warning which he provided give no hint that he had gone over, indeed the nature of what he told me and the risk he took in identifying himself supports that view."

" Can you tell me how you've come to the conclusion that he is dead?"

" I am afraid I cannot reveal that at the moment."

Emnie was getting no further forward. Talking to Scott was not what he had come for, presumably Primrose was not there and without him Emnie was unlikely to achieve any satisfaction.

" You must excuse me, but I have a meeting due to take place here very shortly."

Emnie nodded; there was no value in prolonging the discussion. He finished his drink and rose to leave, when he heard the bell ring twice. A moment later Primrose joined them.

" Good evening, Mr. Emnie."

" Where is Clive Floydd?"

Primrose looked with surprise at Emnie; for an instant he assumed that Emnie was officially concerned. The slight movement of Scott's head halted him before he had done more than lick his lips. Scott now took control of the conversation.

" I am sure Mr. Trewen will be happy to talk to you tomorrow about this."

A direct accusation was the only means left open to Emnie and he used it without hesitation.

" Why did you kill Floydd?"

" I haven't done anything of the kind. I've probably not been within a quarter of a mile of him all day, despite my efforts."

" You have been looking for him then?"

Primrose saw Scott nod for him to continue. There was no point in avoiding the confrontation and every reason to learn the nature of Emnie's information.

" I've been searching between Waterloo, Westminster and Whitehall. I've concentrated on the roads, checking with newsvendors, loungers and the police on duty."

" Did you make any checks on the parks?"

" No. I had no one else to help me and it would have been an impossible task on my own. It would have consumed valuable time, with no certainty of success."

Primrose looked hopefully at Scott's glass, but Scott ignored him, preferring to question Emnie.

" Presumably your information indicates that he was in one of the parks."

" Yes, he was murdered in St. James's Park."

The fact that Scott had allowed the conversation to continue, made it clear to Emnie that Primrose had not been under orders to kill Floydd. He had clearly done it for his own reasons.

" He was murdered by someone who was very keen to determine where he had been for the past eight years and whether he had been in the hands of another government. I am equally determined to find out who was responsible for his being savagely beaten, then killed."

The strength of Emnie's emotion was obvious and Scott probed again.

" You are certain that he's dead?"

" Yes, I'm equally certain that he was responsible."

The bell rang four times, as Emnie glared at Primrose.

Emnie was not sure whether the noise accentuated or lowered the tension in the room. He was keyed up and had been made to surrender much of his information in order to force his way to this point.

The door bell began to ring again and the tension now dissipated appreciably. Scott went into the hall, checked through the spy glass in the door and that hidden in the woodwork beside the front door, found that Trewen was alone and let him in.

Scott detained him inside the door and briefly explained the position.

Trewen came into the lounge and nodded to Emnie and Primrose, turned to Scott and asked him to go with Primrose into one of the bedrooms for a few minutes. Trewen sat down, obviously concerned to set a low key for the beginning of the discussion. He waved to the chair in which Emnie had been sitting earlier and Emnie resumed his seat.

" I'm surprised to find you here, Roger. I had imagined

you had gone home long since."

" I wanted to find out whether CS had anything to do with Floydd's death."

" You know, Roger, I did make it clear earlier and you know very well that this matter has passed out of your hands and that, as the person in charge, I wished you to take no further interest. It seems to me that you are involving yourself. At the moment I am not certain whether you obtained further information in the past hour, or are reacting in an uncharacteristic and emotional manner.

" What do you know that you have not already told me, Roger. I cannot believe that your presence here and your sudden discovery of vital work earlier this evening are unrelated."

" I wasn't in my room this evening. When we were in the control room, I saw Floydd on one of the monitors. I was concerned by your having told me his presence in London was known and I decided that I must get to him before anyone else did. I arranged for a secure room, so that I could bring him back for questioning and hoped to ensure that he was safe.

" When I reached the park, I couldn't find him and only after some time did I find him. He was just alive and no more. He was dying from the effects of a bad beating and an injection."

" Did he say who had done it ?"

" No, he didn't get that far, but he was convinced that I had put the two men onto him. He seemed to think I alerted somebody before I met him today. I did tell you and this has been the result. Primrose was assigned to look for him and is responsible for this. It certainly explains Floydd's conviction that I was involved."

" It represents singularly little to go on and your failure

to tell me all this earlier suggests you've decided you should personally set matters right, which is unacceptable. Did Floydd have any papers on him which could identify him?"

" I think not. I took the papers he had in his jacket and I have them here. You may see them if you wish."

" Roger, the Prime Minister is aware that CS are acting in this matter. He is concerned for reasons of the highest interest that overt interference should not take place with a member of the CIA. It is imperative that you abandon your involvement in this affair and I want you to remain here for the night. Phone Anne if you wish, but do not alarm her needlessly; it is only a question of the next few hours."

Nothing Trewen had said reduced the concern Emnie felt. The involvement of the Prime Minister and the failure to interfere with Fransen only increased his worry. He could not accept that Primrose was innocent of Floydd's murder.

Emnie nodded; he had no alternative but to agree to stay.

" Please go into the second bedroom on the right, while I speak to Scott."

As Emnie left the room, he picked up the receiver, buzzed the extension in the first bedroom and asked Scott to come in.

" Have you found out where Primrose has been during the day?"

" He's been in the area Waterloo to Buckingham Palace. He phoned in regularly and we have a few situations which could provide corroboration, when we have the chance to check them out."

"Do you know where he was from eight o'clock onwards?"

" Yes, he was in our control room. He wanted to watch

the monitors, thinking he could cover a wider area at a time when the light was fading and our infra-red facility would make faces fairly clearly visible. The log has been checked and he arrived at eight sixteen, which is a few minutes after you and Emnie were logged out."

" How many minutes exactly?"

" Four."

Trewen told Scott to call back Primrose and Emnie and the four sat down together.

" It is quite clear Primrose could not have been involved in Floydd's death, Roger. He entered the control room within five minutes of you and I leaving and, from the brief details I have on Floydd's death, he could hardly have covered the ground in the time, far less have been instrumental in the killing.

" I would like you and Primrose to remain here overnight. Scott and I will be concerned with other matters and I would like you both to wait here until you hear from me in the morning. We are involved in a matter of some delicacy and that must outweigh our personal feelings for the time being."

TWENTY

Trewen had to wait for ten minutes in the anteroom before the Prime Minister called for him. He had made up his mind to assess the old man's mood before determining how much detail he should put forward. He continued to be troubled that no restriction of Fransen's movements had been approved. The absence of an attempt the previous night had not diminished his apprehension.

He had become aware of the document which had been prepared and presented to the Prime Minister the night before. Trewen hoped it would have convinced him that the demise of the President could only result in a continuation of the present American policy, or even one still more damaging to Britain's interests.

The Prime Minister was standing with his back to the window and a splendid smile on his face. Trewen felt this was a good start, but as the old man began, he appreciated that it represented self-satisfaction, rather than welcome or pleasure at seeing Trewen.

" Good morning, Charles, do sit down. The President appears to have spent an uneventful night, thanks to the vigilance of his British friends and I am sure he will wish to voice his pleasure that his safety should be foremost in our minds.

" I trust that nothing untoward has occurred since we last spoke and that no new problems have arisen. I presume

Fransen has been watched and permitted to proceed un-impeded, as I required."

"Your instructions have been followed, Prime Minister. Fransen has not taken any unlawful step of which we are aware. Might I ask whether you remain convinced that the Vice-President and his advisers would provide a more satis-factory leadership."

"My assessment would be that the Vice-President is un-likely to follow slavishly the policies of the present incum-bent, Trewen. He appears to share his desire to be popular and has shown no clear indication that he has either the intellect or the ability to establish a definite, considered policy at this juncture. For us this means he could well be influenced by statesmen of experience and that he may look to his principal allies."

"While we have learned nothing further of value on Fransen's intentions, we have no reason to assume that he will not make at attack on the President. Equally nothing positive has come forward to prove that he will do so."

"I would appreciate your apprising me of all the major factors which could influence my decision."

The old man seated himself at the desk, leaning forward, his hands clasped, all traces of his smile gone now and clearly determined to ensure that nothing material was omitted.

"Floydd was killed last night in St. James's Park. It is unclear whether this was done by the Russians, Fransen or the CIA. There is no direct evidence to connect any of them with his death."

"Regrettably, Emnie of Junction, who told me of the contact made by Floydd with him, has allowed himself to become involved in this affair. He was with Floydd when he died. He did not identify his killers and Emnie has shown a desire to ensure that the murderers are identified and punished."

" I trust there will be no startling headlines in the papers about the fourth man in the Philby affair. It would be unfortunate were the names of these two men, who were looked at carefully after the defection, to be linked at this time."

" I have every reason to believe that Floydd's death will be taken to have been the result of a brawl and it appears unlikely that a routine check would reveal his identity. He took great pains to ensure his anonymity when he disappeared."

" And Emnie; I trust you have made sure he understands he should take no further part."

" Yes, this has been made clear and, in view of his troubled state of mind, he was asked to remain in the CS operational flat, until I make contact today."

" There seems no reason for us to believe that the death of Floydd is directly concerned with Fransen or his possible activity. Emnie must continue with his work and drop this whole line. Make that clear to him."

" May I make some direct move to prevent Fransen making an attempt on the President's life?"

" My dear Trewen, you have yourself said that there is as yet no evidence that Fransen will do so. I do not feel inclined to issue instructions for you to impede a member of the CIA. That could be regarded as an interference in a matter of domestic concern to the American government and further, it could place a needless impediment in the way of future, harmonious relations with the CIA. You have on other occasions stressed the danger of our receiving an unreasonably poor response from them. I doubt that anyone could prove Fransen intends to make any attack.

" I see no need to look into the death of Floydd; you seem satisfied that it will go unremarked. We may consider whether an effort should be made to discover who was responsible, after the conclusion of the presidential visit. For the time being, we shall not involve the security services, since this would focus unreasonable attention on Floydd's warning to Emnie.

" I would not wish this Government to be placed in a position where it appeared actively to condone an act against the person of the head of a friendly state. I must however judge what is in the best overall interests of this nation and it is my view that the President's policies are a danger to the whole of the West and most particularly they endanger our economy and the defence of this country. My duty, as head of Her Majesty's Government, is to ensure that the interests of this nation are fostered and not simply to indulge the perpetuation in office of a man, hungry for continued political power, whose actions endanger the free world."

TWENTY-ONE

Emnie awoke with a start. He had been having a particularly vivid dream and he lay for a moment on the bed before he recognised the surroundings and the figure standing in the doorway. Light filtered into the passageway from the lounge and Primrose was visible only in outline, at the door of the second bedroom.

" What are you doing here?"

" The lounge door was open, otherwise I wouldn't have heard you. For a while I thought you had someone in here, you made so much noise."

Emnie continued to look puzzled, as Primrose began to make use of what he had heard him saying in his sleep, hoping to spur him into further revelations.

" You made contact with Floydd and he told you about Fransen."

" Close the door and go away. If you have any sense, Primrose, you'll get some sleep yourself."

The suggestion irritated Primrose, he had wished his intrusion to appear as solicitude, rather than an effort to learn more about Emnie. He had been enjoying a couple of drinks before turning in and the implication that he had been sitting up drinking needled him.

" I don't fancy ever having to share a hotel room with you; your wife can't get much sleep if you always talk in your sleep."

With the most effective parting comment of which he could think, Primrose closed the door and returned to the lounge. He slumped into the armchair just inside the door and picked up his drink, determined to finish it before he turned in. The lounge door remained open; if there was something interesting to hear, he wanted to make certain he was privy to it.

Emnie lay awake, stretched out on the bed, having removed only his jacket, shoes and trousers. He looked at his watch and realised that less than an hour had passed since Scott and Trewen left.

Floydd's comment about the flower continued to perplex him. He began to convince himself that he had misunderstood those last words. Even if he had said flower, it could have been some trick Floydd's mind had played on him after the brutal beating. Emnie went back to thinking of words similar to flower which he could have meant. As he lay there, the fatigue of a day of unaccustomed violence asserted itself and again he slept.

✱   ✱   ✱

Emnie awoke, his mind clear; as he had slept his mind had thrown up the answer to the whole puzzle. He checked his watch and found to his surprise that it was almost seven o'clock. He listened and heard no sound in the flat.

He arose and put on his clothes and opened the bedroom door quietly, noting the light from the lounge.

Primrose was still there and he stood looking at his tousled head, lolling on his shoulder. Emnie decided to close the lounge door, so that Primrose would not hear him opening the front door.

Emnie pulled the door shut. He had turned the handle to prevent the tongue of the lock clicking against the guard, but as the door finally moved into the frame, the tongue engaged, emitting a click, which to his tense senses seemed certain to wake Primrose.

Waiting to see the effect of the noise did not enter his mind, so great was the compulsion to leave the flat. Emnie was at the front door when he heard Primrose's sleepy voice and he turned to see him standing in the doorway.

"Trewen told us both to stay here and I'm damn sure he'd drop on me like a ton of bricks, if he found me here and you gone."

"Mr. Trewen asked me to remain, but I am quite certain he did not place you in control of my movements. I have a very important matter to which I must attend, without delay."

"Then come back into the room, while I phone to check the position."

Primrose moved towards Emnie as he stood in the hall, with the door of the kitchen slightly open beside him. As Primrose reached him, Emnie thrust out both hands, seizing Primrose's arms and swinging him sideways towards the kitchen door.

The move took Primrose completely by surprise, still fuddled by his lack of sleep. As his body hit the door, smashing it wide open, he lost his balance and his feet skidded on the vinyl floor covering. His feet shot into the air and he came down on his spine, his head thudding against the cupboard just inside the kitchen. He lay quite still and was obviously unconscious.

Emnie slammed the kitchen door shut, turned the key in the lock, throwing it behind him onto the carpet and went back to the front door. He opened it with caution, found no one visible and decided to use the stairs, stumbling down them, almost falling in his desire to get to the car rapidly.

TWENTY-TWO

Only fifteen minutes later, Emnie pulled up outside his own flat. He left the car in the road and entered; the pressure to get it over was still insupportable, but he decided to give himself a few more minutes thought and began to walk up the stairs. He realized his stupidity after three flights, when he felt again the constriction of his chest and the palpitation which accompanied it. He waited for a few minutes until it began to dissipate, then climbed slowly upward.

He entered the flat and went to their bedroom to find Anne asleep, the sunlight penetrating the curtains and giving the room a fresh appearance. Looking into the mirror, Emnie realized how bedraggled he looked. His hands went up to straighten his tie and to smooth his hair into some semblance of order. Looking at his face, he saw eyes he did not recognise, reflecting the violence through which he had passed during the past hours. The horror of Floydd's death and his own aggression towards Primrose showed in the hard unseeing quality of his eyes.

" Why are you standing there?"

Anne's voice behind him almost made him jump. In the mirror he watched her ease herself into a sitting position, her head against the headboard and the shoulder strap of her blue, frothy nightdress poised on the point of her shoulder. She looked angry and glanced at the alarm clock to confirm her sense of aggravation.

" Early morning escapades seem to be the order of the week. Where have you been all night?"

" I've been trying to make sure that the proper price is paid for a singularly unlovely act and possibly also. . . ."

Emnie stopped. Talking in the abstract would not help; he must hear the answers to his questions.

" Who did you phone, after I left here yesterday morning, Anne?"

Anne shook her head and busied herself with the pillows.

" I don't know what you mean, Roger, you behaved strangely all yesterday. You race out at crack of dawn, taking the car, you stand up Diana, Charles and me, you send me home in a cab, having decided to go off on some wild-goose chase or assignation. Finally you arrive home, come crashing in here and begin catechising me."

She enunciated perfectly, almost pedantically, as though talking to a racalcitrant child with whom it was difficult to be patient and who clearly deserved neither understanding nor consideration.

" This is not a trifling domestic issue, Anne."

" I have no idea what you mean."

Her mouth had suddenly gone dry. This was not a situation out of which it would be possible for her to bluster her way. Roger's manner showed a resolution he seldom practised towards her. For an instant she glimpsed the qualities which made him so valuable at Junction.

" Clive gave me the clue. You passed the information on Philby, you heard it when I talked in my sleep. You've made me the fourth man."

" Can we carry on this conversation in a civilised manner. I know Fascist states practise arrest and interrogation during the night, but I'd not expected that from you in my own home. Shall we make some tea and do whatever talking you feel is necessary."

As she spoke, her clear, cold tones convinced her she had passed the worst moment and might be able to establish her ascendancy.

" No, we shall talk now, or if you prefer to procrastinate, I'll begin by telling you what's been happening. When Clive Floydd phoned me, you heard me mention his name and where I was going to meet him. You immediately phoned your friends, enabling them to follow him and last night they beat him brutally and then killed him. Before he died, he told me you were responsible. He remembered that ridiculous incident you told everyone about; when you refused to accept delivery of the flowers for Mrs. Anemone just after we were married, not realising the florist had taken a telephone order and that your name sounds identical. You knew your friends were keen to get hold of Clive, or rather to eliminate him and you are as responsible for his death as the animals who murdered him."

Anne remained silent, looking at him levelly. Inwardly she was in turmoil. She was unnerved by the hard, ineluctable manner in which her husband put forward his accusation and by the fixed, unblinking stare focussed on her.

" You've been passing on information for quite a while; why, I don't know. You've chosen to sleep beside me and learn from my night talking odd pieces of information and names; it's small wonder they thought I'd warned Burgess, Maclean and Philby. Their names were known to me as KGB agents shortly before they defected. I don't know whether you warned the first two, as Philby may have done that, but I'm damn sure you picked up the information on Philby from me. How much you passed on I'll never be able to prove, but your sympathy when I had bad nightmares and your desire to continue sleeping in the same bed and to convince me that I was not disturbing you was obviously feigned to preserve your source of information."

He stopped, realising that he had not yet made her react; only an all out attack stood any chance of success.

"Your whole life has been an act. For the past twelve years you've used our marriage to satisfy your desire to destroy this country. You must be incapable of any genuine feeling. In your squalid way you've accepted all the benefits and for some financial or sexual gratification, you've helped this country's enemies."

Anne threw back the covers and stood up, facing Roger, her eyes blazing. Some word or phrase had hit her at last and her control, preserved for so many years, vanished in the rage inspired by her husband's attack.

"How could you ever have thought I was truly interested in you. For years I searched for a way of contributing to the cause and doing something effective to change the clapped-out system you call democracy. Certainly I've used you and the fragments I've pieced together from your mumblings. Through living with you I've been able to give valuable information to our people. Some of it I pieced together; on important subjects they gave me some pieces of the jigsaw, so that I could watch for a single name or word. It's given me a feeling of belonging and doing something truly worthwhile. I was the vital link, taking your mumblings and with some other intelligence, putting it all together so that a valuable man could be warned, or a hint given that your people were about to make some move. For a while I thought they were going to move you from Junction, after they went after you in the Philby investigation."

She was panting now with the vehemence of her feelings and her scorn for her husband. She had blown it, but in her battle with Emnie she was winning. She wondered whether he would ever be able to admit the true situation to anybody. She knew she was bringing home her scorn and anger to him, his expression had changed, fatigue showed in his face and posture, a look of stupefaction had spread onto his features and he was no longer in control of them.

" When Philby went over, you thought I was showing a loving interest in you and, despite your distress at the investigation, you found the opportunity to show me little attentions. Your vanity was such that you thought I was doing it for love of you. In reality I was safeguarding my investment. If you'd been removed from Junction, put out into the wilderness, my four years of investment in you would have been thrown away. Small wonder I buoyed you up, without your position I would have been a failure."

" Then for you, all this has been the acting out of a role you were assigned and had actively sought. Your contempt for me must have been limitless, to have convinced me of your love, to gain some access to my circle and then to discover a final dividend as I began to give you odd names and facts in my sleep. That must have given you star status and to be able to stay on after warning Philby; that must have made them love you. Your life has been a sham. . . ."

The pain in his chest had grown as he spoke. One moment he was upright pouring out his scorn on her, having forced her out into the open, the next he lay on the carpet at her feet, his right arm under his body and his left hand just touching her foot.

His whole side was numbed, he tried to speak and found he was making an awful babbling sound; his lips and facial muscles were no longer under control. From his throat he managed to say the first sound of the word help, but he found he could not shape the words with his lips.

Another spasm shook him as he lay there and now he found he could do nothing; saliva was dribbling from the corner of his mouth onto the carpet, control totally gone, his brain just working well enough to tell him that with or without help he would shortly be finished. He became conscious that he was alone.

Anne had stepped over his body and walked through to the kitchen. She picked up the kettle and took it to the tap, but realising how badly her hand was shaking, she put it down, went to the bathroom cabinet, took out a vallium tablet and washed it down with a mouthful of water from the tooth glass.

Slowly she made the tea and sat down to drink it, black, with only a spot of sugar. Having finished her tea, she put the cup onto the draining-board and walked back into the bedroom. She looked carefully at her husband, without touching him and satisfied herself that he was quite still.

Now she was completely calm and she went into the sitting-room and picked up the telephone.

" He's dead, a heart attack, he had realised my connection. He may have told others of his suspicion and it seems that the man I mentioned yesterday indicated my involvement before he died. You must decide whether it is safe and valuable for me to remain here. I am about to call the doctor. Contact me later in the day."

" Certainly. It is essential that you do nothing to excite suspicion at this stage."

The voice at the other end of the line was equally calm.

Anne checked a number, having replaced the receiver, then dialled.

" Doctor, I'm sorry to trouble you so early, but my husband appears to have had a heart attack. I think he's dead."

TWENTY-THREE

Trewen's car drew up alongside the Emnies' flat and he went to the lift and pressed the bell.

On leaving the Prime Minister, two phone calls had come through for him almost simultaneously. The first from Primrose was in progress when the second call reached his secretary. Consequently, on the second he had only received a message.

Primrose had related the events of the early morning. He was acutely embarrassed by having been caught off-guard by Emnie. He had impressed on Trewen that Emnie was under some irrational compulsion to leave, which caused him to behave in a far more aggressive manner than anyone could reasonably have expected. Emnie's talking in his sleep was also passed on, with the suggestion that Emnie's background be checked for extra-marital attachments, which could represent a security hazard.

Trewen did not particularly like what he had seen of Primrose and felt he could be reacting to Emnie's accusation. When Primrose asked for permission to trace Emnie and maintain surveillance, Trewen told him to contact Scott, seeing his secretary flashing to indicate another call on the line. He found he was too late and learned that Anne Emnie had asked that he come to their home without delay, as something serious had happened.

Before he could raise his hand to the bell, he heard a

murmur of voices and the door swung open. The bag, the clothes and manner of the man who opened the door, left him in no doubt that Emnie was dead. There were words of reassurance, the suggestion that she take tablets he had left. The doctor nodded to Trewen and crossed to the lift.

Anne extended her hands to him, poised and clear-eyed. Trewen examined her face and bearing closely as he walked into the hall. Anne showed her normal assurance and it was clear to him that the full effect of her husband's death had not yet hit her.

" Roger is dead. He had a multiple heart attack and the doctor could not do anything for him. He doubts that he would have been able to do much, even if he had been here at the time."

" I'm so sorry, Anne, you must be feeling terrible. It was very good of you to let me know so promptly. Do I smell some coffee?"

" Yes, come through and we can talk. I'll get another cup."

Trewen sat down in an armchair, having made sure that the sunlight would not be in his eyes or Anne's.

When she returned with his cup, she resumed her seat behind the coffee tray and, knowing his tastes, poured him black coffee and offered him no sugar. She helped herself to another cup of coffee and sat looking at him over it, as she held it in her hand. Trewen knew there would never be a better time to find out what had taken place.

" Had Roger a warning of any sort that he might have a heart attack? I presume his annual medicals had not shown it."

" Once or twice they did show up a spot of high blood pressure, but he was very good about getting it under control and we had not regarded it as a threat, although the doctor did warn him that he would run the risk of a heart attack, if he didn't keep the level down. Roger took his work seriously, as you know, and that placed some strain on him at times."

"How did he seem yesterday? Was he under pressure, did you think?"

"He certainly was concerned. He had a phone call first thing in the morning and, as you know, he didn't join us to watch Beating Retreat. Afterwards, he didn't bring me home or come home himself at all. He appeared this morning and had the heart attack."

"Roger had involved himself in a matter outside his responsibility and continued to interest himself in it after he had handed over the handling of it."

Trewen knew that Anne was aware of the broad scope of Roger's work, although to others it was portrayed as a somewhat prosaic civil service job.

"He was causing us some embarrassment and I had asked him to remain at another location, after he had gone there without invitation. Unfortunately, he did not do so and was determined for some reason to get away and come back here."

Trewen paused, staring searchingly at Anne.

"Why did he come back here in such a hurry, Anne?"

"I really don't have any idea, Charles. He said almost nothing before the heart attack. He offered no explanation for his behaviour, or his absence."

"How long had Roger been talking in his sleep?"

Trewen broke across the thread of their conversation and noted that Anne's eyes swung away from him and she stared out of the window, as she began to answer his question.

"It happens only infrequently; only when he is seriously worried about something."

She brought her eyes back to him and she knew she could not avoid the basic question.

" He seems to have done it for years, certainly ever since we were married. Does it have any significance, Charles? Surely it can't have had anything to do with his death."

" There's a possibility of a security leak through Roger. At the moment it's no more than a theory, but there may have to be an enquiry of some sort. It would be more satisfactory to clear up the whole thing now, to make sure it does not emerge later at some equally painful time. Some part of it goes back to the Philby affair and how he knew at what moment he was about to be uncovered as a KGB agent. A week later he would not have been able to go over. The enquiry will mean Roger's connections and those of his friends being very closely examined."

Trewen sensed that he had got through to Anne. Her normal reserve and poise was not as obvious as they had been when he arrived; her ability to stand back from a discussion and dominate it by the use of her intellect and detachment had been checked.

Anne's eyes moved to the window again. Trewen had shown that he knew a great deal; it was vital that the possibility of her having gained information from Roger was kept in a low key and that no needless checks were made on her associations, even though they were likely to be shown to be entirely innocent. She was determined that her usefulness to the cause should not be limited by Roger's death. Given careful handling, she might be able to operate again. She was after all now a part of the social structure in which senior civil servants moved.

Her newly established determination to remain in the area she had so effectively penetrated, spurred her on to deflect any possible suspicion from herself. If she demonstrated her ability to survive, she might be able to prevent a decision being made to withdraw her. Since speaking to her control, she had developed increasing conviction of her competence to remain a valuable source.

" I am certain Roger was never connected with Philby. I don't know precisely what information he had access to, but I doubt that it was a suitable source for Philby and that would suggest that there was some other informant in a similar position providing intelligence. In any case I'm absolutely convinced of Roger's loyalty and I know he didn't have extra-marital affaires which could have led to a leak."

He could not help being impressed by the clarity of her thought, at a time when her mind must be disturbed to some degree by the events of the morning. She had put up a very complete answer. At that moment he had no intention of pursuing the question of Emnie having slept regularly with someone who might have passed on the information.

It was the strength and completeness of her rebuttal that made it more than a bereaved wife's defence of her husband. She had also said something very significant. That Emnie had not known enough to keep Philby informed. Trewen had not mentioned that Philby had been more than warned when to go over. Only in the past four weeks had the suggestion that he had been receiving regular information arisen, as a result of the defection of a KGB man. That information had been confined to eight people, of whom Emnie was not one.

Anne's confidence of the extent of her husband's knowledge was a tacit admission that she had heard a good deal of Emnie's sleep talking. Trewen made a mental note to examine her security file, which would have been opened on her engagement to Emnie, although she would not have been positively vetted unless some feature of her background demanded it.

"I'm sure that your confidence in Roger's honour and fidelity is entirely correct, Anne, but I am a little surprised that he knew too little to have been involved. It's an academic point if he can be eliminated as a source, but. . . ."

"Charles, I don't pretend to know all he knew, but you can be sure I was kept awake by his talking in his sleep at times and I cannot believe he knew enough to supply someone who wanted hard information."

"I'm sure you are right, Anne and the question only arises if one doubts Roger's loyalty. What I must ask you to let me do is to have a brief look at his papers, while I'm here; it will prevent someone having to come round in the next few days, when I'm sure you won't be wanting someone strange about the place."

"Certainly, Charles. How considerate of you to have thought of it. Roger used the desk in the study; the drawer on the right contains papers to which we might both need access. The other drawer has a filing system, the key is on his key ring. . . . Shall I. . . ."

"That's quite all right, Anne, I'll go into the room and get the key."

Anne led him as far as the bedroom door and Trewen went in, to find Emnie stretched out on the bed. He closed the door and rapidly checked the body for signs of blood and the wrists for marks of an injection. Trewen emptied his pockets onto the dressing-table top, finding the packet of pound notes and the crumpled papers from Floydd. He slipped Emnie's diary into his pocket, then carried out the keys, the money and the papers.

"Anne, I'll take the keys into the study. The money and the papers relate to an official matter. Naturally I will be

137

pleased to give you a receipt, but the money was drawn out yesterday by Roger on his personal charge."

"That's not necessary, Charles. Do go through to the study and make yourself comfortable."

He went into the study and unlocked the left drawer, but chose first to run through the files in the right drawer. He found nothing of significance; the balances of the bank accounts were not exceptional and no substantial receipts or payments were recorded. The files in the left drawer, he was able to move through rapidly and ten minutes later he reappeared in the sitting-room, with only one file.

"Might I take this file with me, Anne, it contains among other things a record of Roger's movements and it would be a great help in determining that his movements don't correlate with Philby's."

Anne's movements were also recorded, but he chose not to mention that. It was in the form of a travel diary and Trewen had been intrigued to find that they had not travelled together as much as he would have anticipated.

"Certainly, Charles, please do. I want to help you clear Roger's name, no matter how far-fetched I find the suggestion."

"Anne, I would like to be sure you are not left to yourself too much. Have you any close relatives who can help? Would you like me to arrange for Roger to be taken to an undertaker and for Diana to be with you? Better still, would you care to come with me now and to have lunch with Diana at our place?"

"That is so kind, Charles, I would love to spend some time with Diana, provided it's not too much of an imposition."

"Could you write your doctor's name and address on a piece of paper and let me have it, so that I can make the arrangements. I will telephone Diana while you get your things together. Please let me have a set of keys for the flat for people to get in, or may I keep Roger's keys?"

Anne nodded, wrote down the doctor's details and left the room.

TWENTY-FOUR

Trewen asked Scott to join him immediately, having told the driver to take Anne on to his home.

" Primrose took quite a knock from Emnie and I've assigned him to help Therfield in the watch on Fransen. He's showing a great desire to shine after the incident at the flat. Our resources are limited and we can only hope to cope with Fransen's daylight movements. If he chooses to go out in the middle of the night, we can do very little."

" The apparent lack of activity made me think Fransen spotted Therfield and took him for an innocent spin through Covent Garden. He had a series of meals in his room and, although we didn't spot it at the time, he was changing with the waiter and getting out in disguise. We've got the waiter's co-operation now and when he tries to make a move today, Primrose will be waiting to follow in our transport."

Trewen nodded. The failure to spot Fransen's movements had been unfortunate, but was not disastrous.

" If support is necessary for Primrose, I want you to handle it yourself. Both you and Therfield are apparently known to Fransen; I would like you to be ready to act if the need arises and I have a job for Therfield.

" Emnie died of a heart attack soon after reaching home this morning. Anne Emnie is at my home now; this is the name of her doctor, these are the keys to their flat and to Roger Emnie's desk. Arrange for his body to be taken to a suitable undertaker, who should contact Mrs. Emnie to-morrow for instructions. Check with the doctor that he is satisfied regarding the cause of death and is issuing a death certificate to the undertaker. Quite independently, have our man look at the body, just to reassure me that it was a heart attack and not something else. No autopsy at this stage, but make sure the funeral or cremation does not take place before we have decided whether there should be a post mortem.

" Have Therfield look in the desk and the flat generally for papers which may indicate any clandestine activity by either of them. Arrange for the telephone to be monitored by the control room and they are not to overlook logging any numbers which are phoned without answer, the number of times the number rings and so on. Let him watch the flat until she arrives back in case someone else has a key to it. He should transfer his interest to Anne Emnie on her return. Once the presidential visit is over, we can increase the strength of our watch. For the time being we shall have to be satisfied with Therfield's best efforts. Arrange that he locates in the porter's quarters and that he hears of any significant telephone calls.

" Do not tell Therfield that you have this file. You are to have it checked to identify whether there is any coincidence in the movements of either Anne or Roger Emnie with those of Philby. Concentrate on the four years before Philby went over; I want that looked at with the greatest care."

" You want me to look for the actual passing of information, rather than a single warning to leave Beirut. Has the position changed radically in our appreciation of Philby's activities before he defected?"

Trewen was not prepared to be drawn on that subject,

141

where his knowledge was based on classified information and the inadvertent comment of Anne Emnie. Trewen pushed the bundle of notes across the desk, together with the papers from Floydd's pockets.

"I wish only to be sure that we check on Anne and Roger Emnie effectively and it is a possibility we should not overlook. Have these notes examined to determine whether they are those withdrawn by Emnie last night. The Security Officer on duty knows all about it. These papers are probably those taken from Floydd's body last night. Look at them to see whether there is anything of interest, from a purely speculative angle, then see whether they are consistent with his having spent the last eight years in this country without any connection with any other power or agency."

"I quite understand."

Scott knew the discussion was over and began to gather the papers together.

"Your instructions regarding Fransen remain unchanged. No action to be taken unless he places himself outside the law."

TWENTY-FIVE

Fransen pulled the blind across the window and looked out at the fine summer day, few clouds in the sky, the flags flapping gently in the breeze blowing up the Thames. He called room service and ordered a breakfast of coffee, orange juice, scrambled eggs, bacon and toast.

He went through into the bathroom and had a shower, shaved and had just finished cleaning his teeth, when a knock at the door announced the arrival of Jack and the breakfast trolley. He slipped on his light silk dressing-gown and sat in the chair placed by Jack in front of the trolley. Fransen sipped the orange juice, while Jack poured his coffee.

"I shall call for lunch at noon, to be served at twelve thirty. I want Frank to bring it up and he can eat it and wait for me to return. There's fifty pounds in it for each of you. If for any reason I'm not back by six this evening, Frank can leave. Come up for this trolley in half an hour, Jack and bring me up a Wall Street Journal when you come."

"Fine, I'll warn Frank that we're on the same run today. He'll be glad to know the rate's improved."

Fransen enjoyed his breakfast and settled down to read the newspaper when Jack returned with it. He had decided not to give his watcher any exercise that morning. He dressed, then put the rifle case on the bed and placed his raincoat and sports jacket on top of it.

The cleaning and checking of his Luger Po8 occupied almost half an hour before he inserted the magazine and placed a round in the breech, putting on the safety catch and screwed on the silencer.

He slipped on the wig, checked it was well groomed, then took up a moustache of Mexican style and applied it to his lip. Experimentally, he blew his nose and wiped his mouth, ensuring that the moustache had remained firmly in place. Then he removed it and put it in his pocket, folded into a second handkerchief. Going back to the bathroom, he removed the wig and placed it beside the other elements of his disguise.

Looking at his watch, he saw it was approaching half-past eleven. He checked the weather again, finding that the sunshine remained, the wind having brought up few clouds. Now he began to go through the items which would remain in the room after he had gone. All the notes he had made were torn into small pieces and flushed down the toilet. The pockets of his clothes were cleared; he felt little regret in leaving these and other items behind, they had served their purpose.

At noon he ordered lunch, then poured a stiff drink and settled in a chair to enjoy it and run through his plans for the day.

*   *   *

The knock on the door preceded the entry of Frank and the trolley. He went to the bathroom and put on his holster and waiter's clothes. He repeated Frank's instructions, picked up the raincoat and jacket placing the case between them and carried them to the door, holding them in front of him, as though he might be taking the garments away for cleaning and making sure that the weight of the concealed rifle case was not shown by the way he held them. Before he opened the door, he held up the Do Not Disturb notice to remind Frank to put it outside.

He halted the lift between floors, took off the white jacket and squashed it into the rifle case with the bow tie. Then he tied his blue tie, put on the sports jacket and raincoat and continued in the service lift to the second floor. There he walked along the corridor carrying the case, entered one of the guest lifts and continued to the foyer of the hotel.

As he moved off in the taxi, he felt no reason to be concerned.

In the taxi behind, Primrose was congratulating himself. The section vehicle had been placed around the corner, so that the driver could watch the service entrance, while Primrose watched the hotel entrance.

The two-way radio was fitted for dual operation, from the driver or the passenger position, with an optional cutout to eliminate the driver, who could listen in when necessary through an ear plug. Tucked away in the driving cab were two coats and a hat, so that a change of appearance could be achieved during a prolonged surveillance.

Primrose called Scott and indicated that Fransen was on the move towards Waterloo Bridge. When Fransen paid off his cab at Waterloo Station, Primrose told the driver to radio that he was following Fransen into the station.

Fransen moved directly to the Left Luggage counter and checked in his case, taking care to mark the receipt. Primrose watched the marking of the ticket, then observed Fransen go to the lavatory and emerge five minutes later with his Mexican moustache, which with the black wig, radically altered Fransen's appearance.

A few minutes afterwards, Fransen was again crossing Waterloo Bridge in a taxi, followed by Primrose at a suitable distance. The cab stopped in Parliament Square and Fransen walked up Whitehall and stood for a couple of minutes at the corner of Downing Street before moving on.

Taking another taxi, he was soon at the Charing Cross Hotel in the Strand enjoying a whisky, while waiting for his cold *consommé* to be brought.

From the forecourt, the section driver indicated his location to Scott and a few moments later relayed the contents of the note Primrose thrust into his hand. Primrose had ensured that Fransen was seated and had ordered a meal before writing down his message.

Primrose went back to the restaurant, secured a table near the door and ordered an omelette, realising as he ate it that he had not eaten a proper meal for two days.

On seeing that Fransen was almost finished, he called for his bill and left the restaurant. Climbing into the taxi, he found that another passenger was already aboard.

TWENTY-SIX

Scott sat well back in the section taxi and told their driver to follow Fransen at a distance. The driver had been busy under the bonnet while waiting on the forecourt and he was now wearing a cloth cap and a blazer.

" Are you quite clear on your instructions, Primrose? You are to apprehend Fransen only if he behaves contrary to the law. If he does so and you are able to hold him at the scene, then you should do so. If a serious situation develops and you are in danger you may shoot, not otherwise."

" I've got it straight. Will I be on this job on my own?"

" If he goes to Downing Street, you will place yourself in the street and get beside him if you can without suspicion. I will be at the corner of Whitehall and our driver will have our vehicle near the steps at the Horse Guards Road end. I've already told him to follow Fransen, if he goes that way and he can't see us in pursuit."

" I don't touch him even if he behaves suspiciously in Downing Street?"

" Correct. Remember he's a member of the CIA in good standing. You must be sure before you act and if he gets away, you glue yourself to his tail and stay there, no matter how cold or hungry you get."

As they spoke their vehicle had moved off, following Fransen's taxi. Fransen left his taxi at the Cenotaph and waited for a gap in the traffic before crossing the road. As he looked down at St. Stephen's Tower, he could see that Big Ben was about to strike a quarter past two.

The section taxi made a U-turn and deposited Scott and Primrose, just after Fransen had disappeared into Downing Street.

Primrose felt there were too few people in Downing Street for adequate cover for him and walked to the steps, watching their vehicle position itself on his side of the road. As more spectators moved into Downing Street, he watched Fransen position himself in the front rank behind the metal barriers. Primrose was intrigued to note that there were no police in the vicinity of the steps, although there were in front of No. 10 and at the Whitehall end.

He assumed that while he was the only man under Scott's control in the street, some of the tourists must be plain-clothes men or CIA agents, as everything could not to be left to the five policemen and the agents who would accompany the President.

The crowd now exceeded a hundred and Primrose sauntered down towards Fransen, deciding to move in close and managing to ease himself alongside him on his right. His work on the files had confirmed that Fransen was a right-handed shot.

As the crowd increased to two hundred, some jostling was taking place, not least by a party of French children to Primrose's right. He stood his ground, then yielded to some pressure, being forced against Fransen, who eased back behind the American couple on the other side of him and who were determined to film the arrival of the President. The husband already had his movie camera out.

Primrose snatched a glance at Fransen from time to time, but he could see no effective way of moving back without

148

making his intention patently obvious. He checked his watch and found that it was almost a quarter to four. Looking around he reckoned that the crowd now exceeded three hundred and he was pleased to see that the constables were preventing further spectators from joining them.

From his vantage point at the corner, Scott had seen Fransen move back to the second rank. Scott could only hope Fransen had not identified Primrose.

Scott stood still, willing Primrose to move back beside Fransen and not aware of the impediment, as some of the children around Primrose were below shoulder level and consequently inconspicuous. He saw Primrose twisting away from Fransen, speaking with a child beside him.

Primrose's effort to make the child understand that he could have his place in the front was a flop and Primrose cursed his failure to master French. The child was determined to remain with his friends and was only conscious of his desire to get a cold drink, which took precedence over any number of world leaders.

As Big Ben was chiming four o'clock, Primrose began watching the entrance to Downing Street, realising he could not effectively monitor Fransen, who was on the other side. He saw Scott's head turn towards Whitehall and after a few seconds heard applause.

*　　　*　　　*

The President left his car, a screen of eight agents having gathered from the cars immediately in front of and behind the presidential limousine. The crowd were delighted to see him so close by and totally ignored the Foreign Secretary and the American Ambassador, as they joined him on the pavement. People rushed to join those clustered in Whitehall and the President went over and began shaking hands, smiling and waving to those further back in the crowd.

The agents were clearly troubled by the glad handing and looked apprehensively from side to side, raising their eyes to the windows of the buildings immediately around them, in no way reassured that these were principally government offices, into most of which entry was strictly controlled. At a word from the Foreign Secretary, the President moved on graciously, conscious that he had a captive audience awaiting him in Downing Street.

Here too he began to shake hands and call out greetings, failing, in his desire to be seen and liked, to notice that the door of No. 10 had opened. Indeed, at that moment he began to turn away towards the television cameramen, who had followed him into Downing Street with their hand-held cameras.

The Prime Minister walked onto the steps of No. 10 and stood smiling, no hint visible in his face or manner of the irritation he felt at this exhibition for the benefit of the voters in the United States. The President turned towards him and began to walk slowly in his direction, ensuring that the newspaper photographers had the maximum opportunity of photographing him, linking his arm through that of the Foreign Secretary as they proceeded.

Finally he reached the Prime Minister, who stood calmly, smiling. They shook hands, saying words that enabled them to appear animated, vigorous and confident. The Press cameramen were now in front of Primrose and the crowd was pressing forward, each person trying to reduce his distance from the men of power. The two politicians stood together while camera shutters clicked and flash bulbs were ignited. The newsmen called for one more picture and Primrose was now sure there would be no attempt. They had misread the situation and the intentions of Fransen.

The American beside him shouted.

"What about one for the amateurs, Mr. President."

Several voices took up the call and cameras were raised in anticipation. The President moved forward, taking the hand of the Prime Minister and gesturing for the benefit of the cameras, as though he were introducing the Prime Minister to his own electors, as though he were teaching him how to reach out to the man in the street, to learn his needs and win his heart.

The calls, the camera noise, the cheers and applause, the excited calls of the French children, completely masked the dull plop.

A look of complete incomprehension replaced the presidential smile; he appeared to stand for several seconds as the red patch spread immediately below the white handkerchief folded in the breast pocket of his blue suit. Then he crumpled slowly to the ground, five yards from the barrier

Fransen threw the gun forward and shoved the American in front of him with all his strength. With his camera raised, he could offer no resistance and was rammed painfully against the barrier. This, together with the crowd pressure, increased by the shock of the sudden collapse of the President, completely upset the stability of the barrier and it fell forward, the front rank of those against it sprawling over it.

The agents were already moving, three stooping over the body, both protecting it with their frames and endeavouring to assess the President's condition.

The others moved beyond the President, only one thinking to shout to the party to get inside No. 10. Each agent had selected his suspected assassin and three of them had assumed that the man who had called out had been responsible, not least because the Luger lay beside him. He was pinned to the ground and one agent had to restrain the man's wife. She had begun to pound the back of the agent who had his knee in her husband's back.

As he lay prone, several children were lying on and around Primrose and it was impossible for him to move more than his head. For some seconds there was a possibility that the crowd behind would continue to press forward, trampling those lying on the ground and exerting pressure on the other barriers, bringing them down.

*　　　*　　　*

As the barrier crashed over, Fransen had begun to ease himself backward, having turned sideways to allow those behind him to press forward on either side of him. Making a raucous noise from his throat, he pushed his way through the crowd towards the steps, calling out that he must have air. Those who were not craning or pushing forward to see what had happened or to observe the actions of the CIA agents and plain-clothes men, were happy to let him pass, being concerned that he should not collapse at their feet. Finally, he reached the steps and walked down them calmly, without hint of panic, nor the suggestion that he was running way. He looked at the park and saw no hindrance to his making his escape through it. The factors against that route were already in his mind, as he reached the foot of the steps and saw the taxi moving towards him with its flag up, for hire. He waved to it and hauled the door open, getting in before it was completely at rest.

" Waterloo Station. How quickly can you get there?"

" At this time of day, it could take half an hour."

" Make it in the best time you can."

Fransen was tempted to offer some overpowering cash reward, but realised that he could be identified later if he made an offer which was too memorable.

The desire to remove his wig and moustache was strong, but he could not do so without being equally conspicuous to the driver on leaving the cab. As they drove along the Strand, a number of factors began to come together in Fransen's mind.

Several times he caught the driver watching him in the mirror. Although there was a radio, he had heard none of the usual messages from dispatchers to their cabs. The driver had an ear-plug and from it there was a wire which certainly did not lead to a hearing-aid and he doubted whether deaf drivers would pass the high standard demanded of London taxi drivers. Finally the taxi had not been cruising when he had first seen it. It had been moving very slowly, possibly moving into position. Now he was not being taken to his destination by the most direct route.

Immediate action was vital; he had already given them the location of his first stop. They were nearing the centre of Waterloo Bridge and Fransen had to get the driver somewhere quiet.

"Take me to the car park for the Festival Hall."

"But you don't...."

"I want to get something from the trunk of my car that's parked there."

When they reached the barrier, the attendant showed some surprise and began to refuse them admission. Fransen interrupted and said his car was parked near the river and the driver set off in that direction. Fortunately there was a space in the farthest row and Fransen told him to park there. As the driver leaned sideways to apply the hand brake, Fransen moved forward, slid the glass partition aside and hit him with the edge of his hand, where the neck met his right shoulder. The driver slumped forward. He looked round carefully and found they had not been observed.

Fransen ripped off the moustache and removed his wig, smoothing his hair into place. Then he left the cab and headed for the pedestrian exit, leading to the Festival Hall. He wound up the tortuous walkway, consuming valuable time. Already half an hour had passed and it would be five minutes more before he could reach the station. He was calmed by the thought that no one knew his luggage was at Waterloo Station and the driver would not be talking for some time, if ever again.

TWENTY-SEVEN

Waterloo Station was crowded. The tempo of the station was reaching its second peak of the day, as commuters began their return to their homes to the south. The crowds provided an element of comfort to Fransen, as he was less conspicuous than might otherwise have been the case. But, when he neared the Left Luggage counter, he cursed them; there was a queue ten long on the retrieval side. Fransen decided he could not afford to wait. He was sure no one could have followed and the driver could not yet have been found, but he did not want any delay.

Fransen went to the head of the queue, as the attendant came back with a bag.

" I've got a train to catch, could. . . ."

" So've we, mate."

The thick-set man third in line was not prepared to have anyone precede him.

" You wait your turn like the rest of us and we won't deport you."

The attendant smiled and shrugged. Fransen cursed himself for failing to blunt his accent and walked to the end of the queue, where the lady at the back said he might stand in front of her, as her train did not leave for some time. This left eight to go and it would take two minutes minimum for each. He was stuck here for a quarter of an hour and it could be a great deal more if a bag had been misplaced.

Finally his turn came and the attendant rapidly produced his case. Fransen inserted the key, which was already in his hand, unlocked and opened it, taking out the sober tweed cap, which he crammed onto his head, snapping the case shut and heading for the taxi rank.

No one was waiting for a cab, the thronging crowd of commuters was bringing with it a plentiful supply of taxis. He took the second cab in the rank and told the driver to take him to the Troy Hotel, having to explain its location.

*　　　*　　　*

The landlady was with Fransen in his room. This was a hotel in name only, six rooms, kettles in each and the offer of meals with the owner. Fransen's room was on the second floor and he looked out at the road below casually, thinking that if she had ever looked like Helen it had been a long time ago and before the bleach was necessary for her hair.

" Yes, yes, Mrs. Troy, I'm quite happy to pay for the two days you held the room for me; I explained that when I booked. One month in advance and you keep that if I leave before then. Have you fixed the bathroom?"

" That's not been easy Mr. Frank, we've only got two bathrooms and loos, so what I've done is put an Out of Order notice on the one down the corridor and told my other guests that I'm waiting for the plumber and they'll have to use the one below. I've locked the door and here's the key."

She gave it to him with a conspiratorial air.

" The phone is not too easy, it's in the dining-room, but we'll try to arrange for you to have some privacy if you need to make a really confidential call. And do let me know

156

if you want anything to eat, that's extra of course, I could bring it up if you want. I don't allow cooking in the bedrooms, just tea or coffee from the kettle."

" Thank you again, Mrs. Troy."

Fransen went over and held the door open for her to leave, which she did with surprising grace, interpreting his gesture as a courtesy and not an attempt to have her go.

Fransen turned the key in the lock gently and swung his case onto the bed. He removed the clothes and got to the equipment which interested him most. He opened a cardboard box and took out his other Luger, checked the action and slotted in a clip, leaving the other magazines in the box. He slipped the Luger into the holster he still wore.

He took the grey-white towel hanging on the chair and laid it on the bed. Onto the towel he put the toilet bag and electric razor, together with another cardboard box. Leaving the case open, he took up the towel by its ends and, putting the dressing-gown over his arm, locked the door, before making his way down a dark passage to the bathroom, with its notice gummed to the figured glass.

Now he was able to remove the cap which he had deliberately bought a size too large, so that he could pull it down to hide as much of his hair as possible. He stripped to his underwear, throwing the clothes he had worn over the edge of the bath.

On top of the low-level lavatory cistern, he spread out the contents of the cardboard box. He took out the razor and opened the moustache trimming attachment.

Ten minutes later the basin was well covered with grey hair. The hair on the top of his head was now less than half an inch long and Fransen inspected the area he had cropped, then picked up one of the passports he had taken from the box, opening it at the page with personal details

157

and the photograph. The shot had been taken wearing an actor's skin piece to simulate the appearance of a bald head and Fransen satisfied himself that the areas were similar.

Taking a tube of depilatory cream from the cistern top, he squeezed a large amount onto his hand and began to massage it into the central part of his scalp. He repeated the treatment, moving outwards and backwards in its application and keeping within the shorn area After about five minutes, it became possible to brush the shortened hair away from his scalp.

Finally he was satisfied and washed the bald patch, which had already altered his appearance substantially. Next he picked up the hair dye, filling the basin and applying the brown tint to the remaining grey hair and his eyebrows.

When he was satisfied with the shade achieved, he washed his hands carefully, having rinsed his hair, then removed his underwear and repeated the operation on his body hair.

He opened the box containing the lenses carefully, removed the clear, soft contact lenses from his blue eyes and inserted the new pair, noting the softening of the colour to grey, with only the faintest hint of blue.

Fransen stood for some time examining his face, confident his appearance now corresponded with that in the passport picture. Then he selected the tweezers from the toilet bag and with considerable grimacing, plucked out the grey hairs protruding from his ears and nostrils.

It took another five minutes for him to identify the aspect of his appearance which seemed out of character and he picked up the razor again and shaved, making a mental note to shave twice a day, so that the light grey stubble would not show clearly at any time.

Switching on the antique geyser, he listened to the comforting hum of the gas burning, as he carefully made sure that no grey hair remained on the floor, in the basin, or at the waste grating of the basin. By then the bath was well filled and Fransen settled into it, relaxing for the first time that day.

For the rest of the day he would ensure that he kept out of the way of Mrs. Troy, in case she had noted his appearance too closely on arrival. He wished her memory of his appearance to fade as much as possible.

In the morning he would assess the desirability of catching the first of the successive flights to Paris on which he was booked. Two were on BEA, one in each of the identities in his two passports and the other by Air France. If he decided not to take the first flight, then he would go on foot to the Victoria and Albert Museum, which would take no more than three or four minutes. His passion for ceramics could be happily pursued for days in the superb collection and he was satisfied he would be safe there.

As he was about to leave the bathroom, he recalled a detail he had failed to handle. He opened the razor and carefully brushed out the compartment beneath the blades, removing the detritus of his grey stubble.

He unlocked the bathroom door, gathered the towel with its load and slung the clothes he had worn over the other arm. All of these would be disposed of before his departure.

TWENTY-EIGHT

By making use of his security pass, Scott forced his way onto the official side of the barriers and reached Primrose as he was rising to his feet. The sheer frustration of being unable to follow Fransen made Primrose tremble as he spoke.

" I think he went down the steps. Did he pass your way? I only hope our driver spotted him."

" He's got away completely; he certainly must have used the steps. Come on, we may get some lead."

They moved as rapidly as possible through the crowd, now penned into Downing Street by uniformed as well as plain-clothes policemen. Instructions had been given that details were required from all those present and that they must wait until transport was available to take them away to make their statements.

Running down the steps, Scott and Primrose could see no sign of the section vehicle.

" I'm going back to the office to see if the driver's checked in and to call him up. Have you any idea where Fransen could have gone?"

The problem that had nagged at the corner of his mind, when he watched Fransen earlier, came back into focus and Primrose knew he almost had the answer.

" When Fransen left that case at Waterloo Station, he marked the ticket. He doesn't seem to have passed it on. Why did he mark it. . . ."

Suddenly Primrose had got it.

"He's got another package at Waterloo and didn't want to ask for the wrong one by mistake. I'm going there."

A taxi was coming towards them as he spoke and he waved at it.

"Ten pounds if you get me to Waterloo without a stop. I'll fix the police if we're stopped."

"I've heard that before, mate, it goes on my record not yours and paying the fine is only part of it. I could lose my licence and where. . . ."

Primrose thrust his security pass under his nose and pulled the door open.

"Get moving and if you wait for me at the station, there's another tenner for you. Now move, this is an emergency; the President's been shot."

*   *   *

There were only two people ahead of Fransen at the Left Luggage counter, when Primrose arrived and felt a wave of relief. He lounged between Fransen and the taxi rank, having fixed a moustache to his lip in the taxi. He had been close to Fransen in Downing Street and this made it more than a piece of vanity. The taxi driver had said he would wait in the taxi line and take him on the following Fransen.

Fransen passed Primrose, heading for the cab rank and Primrose had a moment of panic when he saw his driver was now at the head of the queue. He saw him point to his meter flag, indicating that he already had a fare and gestured at the taxi behind, which Fransen took. Primrose waited until Fransen's taxi was turning out of the forecourt before boarding his cab.

Having seen Fransen's cab stop in front of one of a row

of hotels off the Cromwell Road, Primrose had his taxi drop him round the corner. He walked back, but while he wanted to be sure Fransen was inside, he did not dare enter yet. He must give it five minutes.

Primrose went back to the corner and waited.

The five minutes up, Primrose went up the steps of the Troy Hotel. The hall was not wide and a table beside the door served to accommodate small cards, praising the facilities and naming Mrs. Gladys Troy as the Proprietrix. Also on it was mail not yet collected by the occupants and several dog-eared colour supplements, salvaged from the rooms of departed guests.

He went down the hall and, hearing the sound of un-melodious singing, opened the door at the far end, to find Gladys Troy stirring the unappetizing stew which was sim-mering. She was completely unaware of his presence and this suited his purpose admirably. He pulled a chair from under the kitchen table and sat on its red plastic seat.

" You sing beautifully, Gladys."

Primrose's voice was pitched low, only just discernible over the sounds of the singing and cooking.

Gladys Troy swung round, the spoon clattering to the floor as her hand went to her throat. The moment of shock passed, to be followed by irritation and fear.

" Do sit down, I want to talk to you about something really important."

Primrose took from his pocket the visiting-card and pound notes he had put together while waiting outside.

The sight of the money, the calm manner and the ascend-ancy achieved by the shock of his unsuspected presence, caused her to sit down on the chair on the other side of the table without a word, no longer concerned to dispute his right to be in her kitchen uninvited.

162

" I'm a private enquiry agent and I need your help."

He separated the visiting-card from the money and pushed it across the table to her.

Her eyes followed the card, dwelt on it a moment, then moved back to the money, first estimating the total value, then looking questioningly at Primrose, mutely asking whether she was to receive it immediately or whether she must do something to gain it.

" There's twenty pounds in that pile; in return I want you to answer some questions, without anybody knowing about me. I shall want access to one of the rooms and providing you do as I ask, you'll get ten pounds each day and nobody, not even the tax man, will know about it."

" What do you want to know?"

Her mouth was dry and her voice unusually husky, but her desire to get the money had not been diminished by her lack of saliva.

" I can let you have a room, I've one vacant."

" I don't want a room for myself. I'm going to spend my time down here with you for the time being. The front door makes a good deal of noise when it opens, so if we're quiet in here and keep this door open a bit, we shall hear when anybody goes in or out."

Suiting the action to his words, he got up and opened the door to the passage and left it ajar.

" Now, tell me, is there a way out the back, do you have a fire exit?"

" No, I don't have one; you see, I don't normally have more than six people. The only way out is through the front and out there."

She pointed to the door which led into a pathetic little garden, ending in a blank wall.

" I'm engaged in a very important case and the man who

came in here a little while ago is involved. Do you know what industrial espionage is?"

"Some kind of spying, I think, but Mr. Franks is very respectable. An American or Canadian, I think."

"It means he's stealing a company's secrets, taking away their confidential information and making a lot of money out of other people's hard work. It's rather like someone staying here and leaving without paying the bill."

The parallel got through to Gladys Troy and she shook her shoulders slightly, as though asserting herself in dealing with a recalcitrant guest, who was arguing about the bill.

"Do you know how long Mr. Franks is staying?"

"He's paid for a month in advance, he was due here two days ago and he's going to count those as part of the month."

The thought of ten pounds a day from Primrose captured her imagination, that with the twenty in front of her made over three hundred pounds under the counter. She was beginning to like this strange, confident man; she would do everything she could to make things go smoothly and she was certainly not going to frighten Mr. Franks away, by mentioning this man to him. These thoughts were reflected in the expression on her face and as though as an earnest of her desire to co-operate, she leaned forward to follow the next question.

"Which room has he got, is he going to have meals in?"

"He's got the large room on the second floor, number four and he wanted a bathroom of his own, so I've put the bathroom on that floor out of use and given him the key. He's very clean, I'm sure. You can see the gas on the cooker's gone down, so he's having a bath already; that's extra, of course. I've offered him meals in his room or in the dining-room. He didn't say if he wanted anything. He could be down to use the telephone in the dining-room; no one staying here at the moment eats in, so he wouldn't be disturbed. I don't use the room much since I brought the TV in here."

She nodded her head backwards at the portable monochrome set, opposite the worn fireside chair.

" Well I'm afraid you'll have to give up the telly while he's in, Gladys, because we don't want to miss hearing him if he should go out. You won't mind missing it too much I'm sure. Now, I'm going into the dining-room to make a phone call and I want you to listen for the front door, while I'm on the phone."

Primrose got up and left the kitchen, leaving the money on the table and failing to close the door. As soon as he was out of the room, her hand snaked out and she began to count the money. Reassured that there were twenty pounds, she rose and opened a drawer, slipping the notes into the back of it beneath some envelopes.

TWENTY-NINE

Therfield was well settled in. The porter's quarters were not palatial, but they had a comfortable armchair and the telephone was within easy reach. Sensibly he had taken the opportunity to take a nap; he could not be certain how much sleep there would be for him that night and with Anne Emnie lunching with Mrs. Trewen, she might not be back until half-past three.

The porter was stationed in the hall, with instructions to sound the front bell, when Mrs. Emnie returned, or if someone arrived for her flat. With firmness and courtesy he was ensuring he knew for which flat each visitor was arriving. This was hardly conclusive, but he was taking the precaution of watching the lift indicator, to see whether the visitor went to that floor.

Therfield had already questioned the porter thoroughly about the Emnies, having established himself to be a member of the security services. The porter, an old Scots soldier called Andy Brown, had responded immediately to the stimulus of being involved in a matter graced by reference to the Official Secrets Act.

Brown knew nothing of value about Mrs. Emnie's movements or habits and had observed no regular visitors of particular note. Therfield had then spent two hours examining the flat, without finding anything significant.

Control room had indicated to Therfield that Scott had

no message for him from the papers which he was examining. It had been a long shot to assume that anything valuable could come from the contents of Floydd's pockets and the laboratory were now running over the papers for possible clues to his recent whereabouts.

Every hour Therfield was making a rapid check to see whether the fragment of matchstick he had thrust between the door of the flat and the jamb, near ground level, had dropped to the floor, showing that someone had opened the door. Control room had confirmed that no outward calls had been made. They had however indicated that soon after one o'clock and again at two o'clock, two pairs of inward calls had been made, each set lasting for three rings followed by seven rings. This suggested some prearranged code and they were asked to tell him if any similar calls were made, immediately they occurred. Otherwise, there had been two inward calls, the callers having rung off after eleven rings in one case and nine in the other.

It was almost three o'clock when control room notified him that Anne Emnie was on her way back. Immediately afterwards they called back to say that another pair of the distinctive calls had been made to the flat.

Half an hour later, the porter rang the bell three times, indicating that he had just sent up the lift with Mrs. Emnie in it. Therfield checked briefly with him and found that a taxi had brought her home and been paid off. He phoned control room, warned them of her return and that he was anticipating the four o'clock phone call and going to his car outside, to be ready if she left for a meeting as a result of the call.

Therfield waited in his car until ten past four, then decided he had acted prematurely and phoned control room. A call of three rings had been made followed by another which she answered immediately. They played back the conversation to him, having warned that the meeting was set for five minutes to five.

Therfield heard them positioning the tape.

" Hallo, what number do you want?"

" I think I have the correct number."

The voice was slightly accented, but not a Russian accent or one Therfield associated with Eastern Europe; probably an Arab, he decided.

" All clear, no obvious watch, the porter is over attentive, but he must know about Roger and is probably being sympathetic."

" Come at four fifty-five; don't worry about Brown, he showed no interest when I came back in. Avoid taking calls before you come and I recommend you not to make any."

" I will see you shortly."

Nothing further was said, no location given and it was already four twenty. The man had seen the porter and had not been noted by Brown; that made him a resident.

Therfield went over to the doorway leading to the hall and beckoned Andy Brown over.

" When you showed me the list of residents, I saw no strange names. Are you sure you have no Russians or Eastern Europeans living here?"

" Definitely not."

The Scots accent was clear and the comment precise.

" Then have you any Arabs of any sort?"

" Certainly, Mr. Bakar, he's with one of the Arab embassies, I forget which."

" I don't remember an Arab name on the list, Andy."

" The agents never get it right, they're forever typing Baker; they even put that on his mail box, when they sent down the mail tag and he tells me they always send the rent charge in that name."

" What is Bakar's flat number?"

" Thirty-three."

Therfield moved rapidly to the telephone and contacted control room.

" Get a tap on Bakar, flat thirty-three in this block. I don't know the number, but rush it. That's where the meeting is. Now, give me Mr. Scott."

A few moments later Scott came on the line.

"The President's been shot, we've lost contact with Fransen and I want you to keep an eye open for him. What have you for me, I've seen the conversation transcript."

" There's an Arab in flat thirty-three, I've just asked for a tap. His name's Bakar and is a member of some Arab embassy. It reads to me that his flat is the site for the meeting. There's no way I can listen in. What shall I do and who do I follow if someone leaves? Do I go after Bakar, or do I stick with Mrs. Emnie?"

" Stay with her, don't change your plans, I want to know who she contacts and I want you to get descriptions of any visitors for flat thirty-three, from the porter, as well as those for Anne Emnie. Can you continue through the night, if necessary?"

" I reckon I can keep some sort of watch, but it will probably have to be outside in the car, which means I could be spotted fairly easily."

"Do that and watch out for Fransen, he could come your way and tell the porter to watch out for anyone who could be coming to that meeting."

THIRTY

The door opened immediately Anne tapped on it and she went into the hall. Ahmed Bakar took her hand and held it for a few moments, looking at her with sympathy and a certainty of manner which suggested that he would discover any hint of weakness in her.

"You have been through a great deal, are you able to continue, or do you feel the pressure is too great?"

Already he knew her answer but the question was necessary and the form of her answer important.

Now they were standing in the sitting-room, unremarkable in its furnishings, except for two Bokhara rugs placed on adjoining walls. The heavy red and black added a sober note of colour to the traditional furnishings.

"Having come through this crisis, I now feel able to face anything. I think I should stay in position until some other opportunity comes along. Roger lived a narrower social life than was ideal, more than made up by his value as a source. However, we have friends among senior civil servants, some of them in sensitive areas and a few people we know are MPs. I'm not overexposed socially, which can be an advantage for a new widow on the scene."

"Your fortitude is quite compelling, Anne, but don't you think tradition makes men feel widows are vulnerable, indeed available, my dear?"

"You make a basic assumption about women, justifiable

in someone used only to oriental society and the passive attitude of women, where divorce or the death of a husband can leave the woman largely defenceless, but you are completely familiar with occidental society and your assumption of the role of the hunted for the widow indicates a personal lack of regard for the abilities of women."

"Come, come, Anne. I am concerned for you."

"Then you should not be, Ahmed. I did not devise the idea of marrying Roger from the outset, but when I saw the possibilities, I caused him to propose and I was instrumental in preserving three of our people, one of whom would certainly have cracked under interrogation. Their preservation became a major cause of irritation between the Americans and the British and made the British indulge in a bout of self-examination and recrimination which put them back years in their intelligence work and finally it held them up to the ridicule of the world. The Establishment was shown to be weak and worm-eaten for just the same reasons that it had previously been felt to be strong, by those within it. They were shattered that men of their own kind, men they had worked with or known, or who had pretended to be their friends, had used, deluded and mocked them.

"You came into the picture only when I couldn't meet with Philby with adequate frequency; your position has grown stronger only because you became my control, passing on my information. Now you talk of concern for me; you should be thinking of the area of our greatest need and determining how I can enter it."

"Anne, you could not have more effectively put my fears for your emotional stability into better focus. I am sure if they questioned you, having discovered your true role, you would tell them nothing of value. But I would like to hear whether you have found that Roger shared his suspicion of you with anyone else before he confronted you."

Here Ahmed demonstrated the talent which made him valuable and which Anne was never prepared to recognize. He was not simply a sounding board through which messages to and from Anne could pass, but a man capable of adding valuably to the quality of decisions, by seeking out weak points and making sure that adequate attention was paid to them.

" I don't think Roger had spoken to anybody, but I am convinced that Trewen has some suspicion of the murder of Floydd being directly linked to his contact with Roger. It was a clumsy operation; I presume Nikki handled it. He behaved like the sadistic butcher he is at heart and from that starting point the whole structure has collapsed. Without that incident, I am certain Roger would never have suspected me. Now I have to begin again.

" Charles Trewen also remembered the doubt about Roger after Kim Philby went home. Clearly as he had this suspicion of Roger, it was wise for me to strengthen the feeling that it could have been he who passed information to Kim, diverting attention from me. I've spent several hours with his wife today and I'm sure we can forget that problem."

" But if Roger is regarded, even now it is too late as the Philby source, surely you will be tainted also and that could lead you into a no-man's-land, where you are isolated, an untouchable."

" Not if I choose to become involved with a politician and one with some prospect of becoming a minister. One delight of the British, two-party system is that you are certain to be in office at least once each decade."

" I accept that as a possibility, Anne, but I would like to be certain about the comments about Roger and Philby.

Did you suggest Roger was a source of information and not simply the man who warned Kim?"

Until that moment the stress of that day had hidden this point from her; Ahmed had sought out her area of weakness. Now she showed her scorn for his ability and lied to preserve the image of her usefulness and thereby guarantee a role for her for the future. Only in this way could she fulfil her need to be valued.

" My reference to Roger was oblique, in no way was it an accusation. It was a slip of the tongue, when I said just now that Roger was Kim's source, I was simply making a vague comment, nothing specific, totally unspecific and oblique."

The words, so imprecise, so unlike her precision in reporting conversations and detail and her look of daring confidence, left Ahmed in no doubt that Anne was lying.

The need to lie and the slip she had made in talking with Trewen, irritated Anne and the fact that Ahmed had identified it angered her.

" You must make it clear that no suspicion attaches to me and that I can now take on an even more critical role in the political scene. My background is impeccable and the death of Roger can only create sympathy. I am objective enough to know that I still create the impression which could be interesting to a man of ambition, who also sees in me someone whose intellectual qualities would complement his own and bring to his dinner table the men who must recognise his talents and advance his career."

" Anne, your strength and fortitude is magnificent. You can be sure that I shall pass back your conviction of the validity of the new role you have mapped out and your skill in handling Trewen."

Still he harped on Trewen. Her anger grew stronger and

it moved beyond her control.

" When I establish myself in my new role, Ahmed, I shall require a control more in keeping with the *milieu* in which I shall be operating. You would, I am sure find the vagaries of British politics too complex and confusing, even though you have spent so many years in this country."

Anne saw his face tighten at the insult to his competence and the suggestion that he should carry back the message that he was no longer competent in her estimation. She knew it had not been the moment to make the suggestion, she had allowed her anger to overcome her mind, she had made an enemy of a man who was about to pass on a recommendation on her fitness under stress; no matter how his opinion might be rated, it would nonetheless be given some credence.

" Quite so, my dear, but then I suppose these events will bring changes for all of us. After today, I could well find myself in Washington, who knows?"

Anne felt unsure of herself; he knew something she did not know and he now dominated the meeting, his coolness and control had overcome her intellect and ability for the first time.

" What happened today of such importance?"

" It was not only Roger who died today, Anne. The President was assassinated in Downing Street and the man who did it is still at large; indeed no one seems very clear who was responsible. From my point of view, it could mean some change in the staffing of our embassies, I have already served here for longer than is usual and my activities are hardly those directly encouraged by my government. Yes, I think a move could be a good idea and that could go hand in hand with our finding a suitably eligible control for you, Anne. We must ensure we keep you happy and secure,

Anne, you know so much of value to the cause and which could be of value to our enemies. You talked of the propaganda quality of our three friends' defection. Think of the satisfaction the British would achieve if they could bring you to trial and the embarrassment for us."

Suddenly, the nausea of fear swept over her. Her husband's death had created no appreciable effect; now she experienced the gripping nausea and certainty of her fear.

THIRTY-ONE

Trewen waited in the anteroom while the television equipment was removed from the Prime Minister's study. Although he did not normally smoke a great deal, he felt a strong urge to take out one of the small cheroots, of which he smoked no more than two in a day. Trewen knew the Prime Minister's keen sense of smell would readily discern the aroma of cigar about him and he desisted, wisely for this could be an explosive situation. The old man had just finished what was doubtless an emotional and effective obituary of the limitless merits of the man whose death he had failed to prevent. Trewen had been called to report and now with the time approaching eight o'clock was concerned to be allowed the maximum freedom of action.

He was taken to the Prime Minister, the room having been rearranged and he was waved to a chair, as his master continued to make amendments to a document in front of him. As he waited, Trewen noted the black tie, off-white shirt and dark suit.

"These matters are always most sad, Charles. Few men become head of state without some real virtues, the loss of which must be regretted, but it is the balance between his virtues and his vices or divisive policies which is vital in the final assessment. I am looking forward to developing a thoroughly satisfactory relationship with the new President, who has already been sworn in. I intend that he shall have access to whatever advice and guidance an experienced world leader can offer him. I have been a Cabinet Minister and Prime Minister for far longer than he has been in active politics and I have hopes of a sound relationship developing, in which the true needs of both our countries are kept in a proper perspective and the divisive attitudes and policies of his predecessor put aside. He has an election in a year's time and in a period in which his people will look for stability, he will be well advised to ensure that his allies provide all possible backing and that controversial issues do not needlessly arise."

The Prime Minister leaned back against the hard, wooden spine of his chair, as though to ease himself from the rigidity imposed during his television performance.

" I shall require from you your appreciation of the new initiatives we may take in re-establishing a greater American participation in Western defence costs and I wish you to pay specific attention to the manner in which they must allow us to supply arms into their armaments and defence programmes. For too long the Americans have told us that common weaponry is desirable and economical. It has, with rare exceptions, also proved very profitable to them and they have seldom chosen to buy from us in return, if we exclude aircraft engines and one or two other items.

" I know you have spent some time in these past few days on security matters, but I want these brought to a speedy conclusion and your attention focused on defence questions. Your ideas remember; we'll get the views of the Chiefs of Staff in a few days, by then I want to have thought the whole thing through.

" Now what have you to tell me and how do you recommend that we handle matters?"

" Emnie has died of a heart attack and Fransen is in a

place which we are watching. He was responsible for the killing. I recommend that I should tell the CIA in London where he is hiding and that we should leave Fransen to them. It can be handled in a way which enhances our relationship with them."

"You mentioned Emnie before Fransen. That suggests you regard his death as having more significance than Fransen's location. Why?"

"I have formed the view, Prime Minister, that Emnie was the fourth man. From the information to which we have access, vital leaks on the closing of our net on Burgess and Maclean probably passed to the Russians. Information subsequently passed to Philby, as we know from a valid source and that information also warned Philby when to leave Beirut for Moscow. I am convinced Emnie was the innocent source of that information. Emnie was a poor sleeper and in times of pressure would talk in his sleep. The killing of Floydd, an inclination to incriminate her husband, a knowledge that Philby received regular information as well as a warning and a correlation between her known movements and those of Philby, indicate that she was the fifth person. In the past few hours she has made contact with an Arab diplomat, who could well be her control, or a messenger."

"There must be no further mention of fourth or fifth men or women. You will ensure, Trewen, that no Press speculation is aroused about Emnie or his wife. She must not be allowed to function further."

"Certainly, Prime Minister. Clearly, we cannot allow her to go over. She may have no further information of value, but her appearance in Moscow would be most unfortunate. I have already arranged that a series of calls are made on her, which will indicate an extraordinary interest by us in her. Therfield has been watching her discreetly during the day, but we have now had him call on her twice and also ensured that his surveillance is conspicuous.

"The Arab diplomat is so concerned that in the past two hours he has stopped using his telephone. He has left his flat and probably told his KGB superiors of the surveillance. My feeling is that they will not choose to take her out, but I have already issued an all ports warning to prevent her leaving. One further call will be made on her by Therfield shortly, then he will call again at eight o'clock tomorrow morning. If they do not decide she is a dangerous risk, then we shall take her to a safe house and a decision can then be made on her future. You clearly would not want her to stand trial."

"The Arab diplomat, who is he; were we aware of his sympathies?"

"No. Although it represents a reasonable hypothesis from some of his past connections and it ties in with the fact that Philby was travelling and reporting in the Near and Middle East. I intend advising MI5 of his probable character, without at this stage indicating how we identified him. Probably they will be best advised to watch his future activities, rather than arrange for him to be declared *persona non grata*."

"Your recommendations appear to fulfil my requirement of a speedy conclusion and the improving of our relationship with the CIA is always desirable. Try to avoid the need to take in the Emnie woman; involve someone else if necessary and keep up the overt observation by Therfield."

"I will attend to these matters on the lines laid down, Prime Minister."

THIRTY-TWO

The flickering pictures threw shadows onto the wall and fleetingly illuminated Gladys Troy's face. Neither she nor Primrose had risen to switch on the light and outside it was dark. Her interest in seeing the latest episode in her favourite TV series had proved so great that even Primrose's insistence on no sound had not prevented her from watching. The thrill of this new facet of her life had diminished with the boredom of Primrose's monosyllabic presence. The agony of whether she would get the money was over and she wondered whether it was all worthwhile, as she tried to lip read, becoming more confused as each minute passed, looking up to measure the value of suggesting that putting on the sound a fraction would do no harm.

Primrose got up and looked at his watch, turning its face towards the set, to catch some light. It was almost ten o'clock and he opened the door to the passage wider.

" You can put up the volume now, Gladys. I shall have some visitors in a minute or two. Then you can have it on as loud as you like and I want you to switch to BBC1 at ten o'clock, when this programme's finished."

Primrose had already determined that the pop concert on that channel would provide a higher and more constant noise level than the measured tones of the ITV newsreaders.

" Lock the door, when I go through, we don't want anybody coming up on you silently do we, while you're listening to your programmes."

Gladys Troy turned up the volume and followed Primrose to the door, an expression of martyred resignation on her face. The credits had begun to roll as Primrose had spoken and now the theme music of the series was filling the room.

"Lock the door and change to BBC1, there's a good girl."

Primrose stood briefly, hearing the mortice lock turn and the introductory words for the pop concert. Without switching on a hall light, he went to the front door and opened it gently. It made a good deal of noise, but the sound from the television masked it from those above. He took a colour supplement and jammed it under the front door, to hold it open.

He went to the dining-room and stood in the doorway so that he could see the front door, but able to withdraw into the room if someone came in unexpectedly.

*　　*　　*

Ten minutes later, Rod Starker eased his thick-set body through the front door. A slim, tall young man followed him, their faces in shadow, the only light being shed by the street lights outside. The young man stooped, removed the magazine, closed the door gently and snapped down the latch on the yale lock.

They followed Primrose into the dining-room and he put on the central light, from which two low-powered bulbs shone from a pendant of five lights. They sat down at the bare table.

Pretending to a greater familiarity and ease than was the case, in the hope of impressing the younger man and to cover the initial moments of tension, Primrose began.

" Good to see you again, Rod."

" And you. Where is he?"

" He's on the third floor, in room four. I've kept away from the room, but the landlady checked he was in his room and wanted nothing just after eight. He has the use of the bathroom on that floor, which is marked Out of Order. These are the keys, room door and bathroom, no bolt in the room. Two other rooms on that floor, five is unoccupied and six, the guy hasn't got back yet."

" And the landlady?"

" In the kitchen at the end of the corridor, she has the door locked, that's the only other way out. You'll have to give the old girl some cash tomorrow to cover her lost expectations."

" Right, I want you to stay down here with me. Jim is going up top to bring him down. I'm going to back stop here. If the passages are as narrow as that to the kitchen, then we're better split than getting in each other's way."

Jim nodded his agreement and moved to ease his gun in its holster under his jacket.

" I have a car just down the way and the driver is back stopping the front door, so we shouldn't lose him. I want you to keep the landlady happy after we leave and I'll have someone back here tomorrow, with a bundle of cash. I don't want her in the room. We'll seal it after we leave and if the seal is broken, she gets nothing. We'll clear it out tomorrow, a thorough search tonight could throw up too much noise. And the sealing goes for the bathroom too."

Rod Starker looked at Primrose and Jim in turn and noted their agreement. He walked over to the door and opened it, looked up the staircase and gestured briefly for Jim to go up. He allowed Primrose to remain behind him and when Jim moved up the stairs, he reached back and switched off the dining-room lights.

Jim climbed the stairs to the floor above with the easy grace of a trained athlete, his hand over his heart beside the butt of his Smith and Wesson Magnum. As he climbed the final flight of stairs to Fransen's floor, the gun was in his left hand and the key to the room in the other. There was a light on the staircase but none in the passage and he saw the light showing beneath the door of Fransen's room. To accustom his eyes to the brighter light in Fransen's room, he went back and switched on the passage light.

He stood before the door and inserted the key gently into the mortice lock, relieved that it was not a yale.

The key rotated without any noise and the door was ready to be opened without a sound from within the room. He transferred the gun to his right hand, gently took hold of the door knob and braced himself, taking a deep breath.

The door swung open, Jim stood in the doorway, Fransen was in profile, seated with a book on his knee, his jacket off.

His disguise gave him an unexpected advantage. No one had known of his new appearance. They had been told of a Mexican-style moustache and black hair and Jim had seen his photograph on file. The bald man with some brown hair and faded eyes, the jeans and the suède shoes were unexpected and Jim's training told against him. He looked for a feature to tell him it was Fransen.

Fransen rose, his hand had moved down his right side to the seat of the chair beside him, away from Jim and he pivoted, crouching and firing before he had completed the movement.

He had beaten Jim to the shot. Surprised and off-guard, he had still managed to get in the first shot and it slammed through the breast pocket of Jim's grey suit, hitting his heart.

Jim's finger had taken the first pressure on the trigger as he saw the Luger as Fransen turned and the shock as the bullet hit him tightened the finger, firing the revolver. The impact of Fransen's bullet had brought the barrel of his gun up and the half adopted crouch of Fransen placed the gun directly in line with his face. The bullet smashed into his nose and a large section of his skull was blown away, as the bullet exited.

Seconds later, Starker arrived and took in the scene. He went back to Primrose at the top of the stairs.

" Make sure no one comes up for two minutes, till I get the door closed. Then get the landlady to invite the guests out for a drink at the pub down the way. Tell her she's won fifty pounds on the pools. We'll clear up tonight. And call up our driver, Vince is his name, tell him to call for the truck and five men with cleaning gear."

THIRTY-THREE

Anne was convinced her visitor had come to the wrong flat. Simon's beard was now almost white and his long hair was equally affected by the advance of time. It was over twelve years since they had last met and her life had carried her far away from the world of political discussion and the intense arguments in the Student's Union at London University, where they had first met.

Simon's description of himself in those days was as a perpetual student. He had followed work down the mines as a Bevin boy, during the war, by a degree in history and the diploma in archivy. Finally he had been forced to give up his amateur status on obtaining his PhD. Publishing had followed and, when they both lived in Hampstead, they had met from time to time.

He had provided the stimulus in Anne's movement from a person intellectually attracted by the socialist ethic to someone prepared to dedicate her life to achieving the objectives of the communist state as embodied in Russia. This dedication would never receive recognition publicly and she had accepted that she would have to sustain herself from her personal satisfaction in the work she was to do.

This had led to her being chosen to be placed in Roger's company and inevitably to their marriage.

Simon had not been involved in the final stage and it had been essential that their association should cease. Over the years it had been increasingly important for Anne to appear to have no contacts which suggested an unacceptable background politically. This did not prevent her putting the communist case within her own social circle, but this was done without heat and accepted as being a perception by a clever woman of the merits which existed even in opposing systems.

Simon's role had suited his temperament and he had recruited in the mines for the party and towards the end of his time at the University for the KGB.

It was the element of sacrifice of her own interests which had captured Anne's mind most powerfully. Action without recognition; work whose value she would never learn or be capable of assessing objectively. Some could not continue without the stimulus of recognition or persecution, others failed because they became depressed by the apparent absence of effect from their efforts, or began to overestimate their contribution, demanding new and wider fields of operation, in line with their exaggerated abilities.

*   *   *

" Do come in, Simon."

Anne led him to the sitting-room and looked at him carefully as he sat down.

" Is this a coincidence, Simon? If so, I suggest you leave immediately and please give the impression you were calling on another flat. If it is not, let me warn you that I have been questioned three times today and I could well be under observation."

" I know, Anne. I walked down from the top floor. So much has happened since we last met. Your marriage and now your bereavement. I understand you have been doing very valuable work, although, naturally, I don't know the details.

"Your husband's death is most sad and unfortunate. You show great fortitude in maintaining your bearing. He was a senior civil servant, I believe. No, don't tell me."

Simon held up his hand, he had no wish to know; his instructions had been clear. His selection to come to her had been based on their old association and the fact that he would be a face unfamiliar to those currently around Anne.

"I have achieved some satisfaction from the work I've done, Simon and I hope I shall be given the opportunity to operate in an even more rewarding environment in the future. I've grown used to the discipline which one has to impose on oneself when working in this way and I know I can continue to be effective. Is that the answer which you came to get?"

"Your words have given me much of the answer, but I fear you don't have a clear conception of the position you are in at present and the consequences.

"The interviews and surveillance have not been the only consequence of your actions."

Anne waved her hand and interrupted.

"My action. What do you mean, Simon. You come here and seem to have already accepted the opinions of a man whose experience is scant and whose judgement can't be taken seriously. Anything you've heard of my actions through him is manifestly suspect."

"What would you say of his opinion, if I told you that all ports, airports and airfields have your photograph and description? We have definite confirmation of this. It seems that either you have been under suspicion for some time, or your husband confided his concern regarding your loyalty to someone in authority, or you could have made some comment which has directed suspicion to you.

"You will not have known that a KGB man has gone over. We are virtually certain he did not know your identity. He did however have access to Philby's information relayed into Moscow and from it some deduction may have been possible, or it could be that you have inadvertently revealed to people here that you know information was passed to Philby and not a simple warning to go over."

"That's nonsense, Simon, I simply made a slip of the tongue; in talking to my control, that is."

The anger which had mounted in Anne, suddenly slipped away from her and she felt an awful inevitability about the conversation. They would make no effort to get her out of the country now, as they would not risk her being taken in flight.

"You will have realised I've come to tell you of your next assignment. It is important in preserving the integrity of your past work; it may not be the grander role you had anticipated, but it is important and having watched you grow and mature in your understanding of our cause and the needs of the party, one I know you will understand.

"My dear, I was told to come and see you to tell you of the decision because I have known you so well. My opinion was sought on whether you would undertake the assignment. I was able to reassure them that your loyalty and desire to contribute could not have diminished from those early days in the Students' Union."

Simon reached into his pocket and took out a small, clear tube containing white tablets. He came over to Anne, opened her right hand and put the tube into it, then gently closed her fingers around it.

"You will take a bath, then take all of these; the dose has been carefully calculated, they are the same as you generally have to help you sleep.

" You've made a very valuable contribution to our cause and you have the means to preserve it as a magnificent feat by this further, single act."

Simon turned and walked slowly out of the room, his feet making no sound on the thick carpet. He eased the front door shut, the sound of the door closing echoing in his ears as he began to walk up the stairs.